CW00850673

# Hidden Truths
## Stories of the Akesh

Edited by Stewart Hotston

Cover art by Simon Campbell-Wilson

ISBN-10:1494271133
ISBN-13:978-1494271138

# DEDICATION

Without CP, the people of the Akesh, along with our friends and family, these stories would never have seen the light of day. Thanks for your support and the streams of sambuca. Except the banana sambuca – that can die in a ditch.

# CONTENTS

# ACKNOWLEDGMENTS

Peter Reilly and David Moore from Curious Pastimes, one
for his enthusiasm, the other for his unfailing support.
Si Campbell Wilson for having an eye for images that make
us all happy.
Theresa Derwin, because without her we wouldn't have
attempted this at all.

# FOREWORD

These stories were inspired by two sources of creativity; the first of these is the Live Action Roleplaying system run by Curious Pastimes in which all the people here enjoy dressing up and losing their nerdy selves for whole weekends at a time. The second was the group in which most of the authors were playing at the time these stories were written – The Akesh. Hence the stories themselves are skewed towards this tiny corner of the game. Add to that, most of us are amateur writers who originally penned these shorts for the love of entertaining our fellow players. So, enjoy, but remember, we did this for our own entertainment – hopefully you will enjoy reading our attempts as much as we did writing them.

# 1 A LONG WALK IN THE DESERT
## BY STEWART HOTSTON

"Well that didn't go according to plan."

Shash looked over at Ismar but said nothing. Some of the others muttered their own commentaries but anything they might have been saying was drowned out by the lingering thunder of a falling empire. The dust was everywhere; flakes the size of fingernails, white and silent, drifted through the sky like some absurd parody of frozen rain. Less than a league from the outskirts of Instantine and it was no longer visible, lost to history as well as its own people.

"If there's an Essence of Luck I wonder in what life we screwed his sister in the ass," said Elian An Aster. His comment was greeted only by a sudden gust of howling wind redolent with the creak of collapsing masonry and the lament of a hundred thousand dead souls. Shash wondered if it grieved over such a sundering of creation and he looked at Belloc, but the former Lord of Air was shielding his eyes against the dust storm like the rest of them.

Not daring to pause for too long, lest he be left behind, Shash threw a searching gaze around himself at the survivors. He could see a few hundred feet to his sides but the dust clouds behind them were thick like the coastal fogs of Kadabad. Of the shuffling crowd following in the wake of the five survivors of the Six he could make out just a hundred or so silent bodies concentrating on putting one foot in front of the other. Finding his mouth was dry not just with fragments of dust but the unslakeable thirst of loss, Shash discovered he had nothing more to say. Looking at his feet he wondered what would happen if he stopped willing himself to put one in front of the other.

By nightfall they had travelled another league away from Instantine. Two days ago that would have been close enough to the city to have been embraced by its rolling farmlands. Harvests of maize, corn and canes that had fed the Families of Akesh. The lake upon whose central island Instantine had been founded was gone. The irrigation channels were clogged with dust and all about them only the barest traces of the bread basket of the Kesh remained; a shattered palm stump here, a collapsed windmill there; its blades laying scattered around its base like some tree in autumnal mourning.

They were lucky, as was their way. Ismar, true to his calling as the First of Cyrenus, had smelt out water in the darkening of twilight. The company had stumbled their way to a small oasis whose water was swiftly declared clean. Creation only knew its source but the conflagration which had engulfed everything that morning did not seem to have touched this tiny sprite of life, tucked as it was in a palm shaped hollow leeward of the explosion.

Elian's remaining people had made a count of the other survivors. Three hundred and fifty four. Gathering the other Firsts Elian had reported on the state of their supplies.

"We're buggered," He said, sitting cross legged on a bed of fern leaves, hands steepled in front of his face.

"Perhaps you could be a bit more expansive NaBaal," said Ismar crisply.

Elian regarded Ismar for a moment, as if he were an unaware mantis about to be eaten by a reptile, "We have no supplies. Of the four hundred of us who entered the Circle forty six died protecting the rest of us as we completed the unbinding and dissolution of the Lord of Body."

No one said anything, it was, after all, exactly what they had planned.

"Our supplies, Ismar, were *outside* along with our armies, our horses, camels and everything else! I can get it written down if it would help, you useless moron."

Shash was calmly glad that only the five of them were present. They had retreated a few dozen yards from the oasis to meet. It was bad enough their people had seen their armies evaporated like so much pipe sheesha but they didn't even know the truth of why they were at Instantine in the first place. Elian would probably have spoken this heedlessly in public and, normally, it would have led to blood being spilt to demonstrate appropriate respect.

Instead Ismar shifted on his buttocks and Belloc al Kade tin Macenod coughed to get everyone's attention.

"Unbinding a demon is not an easy process," He

began. There was nervous laughter from the others. "We knew this might not work and we knew resistance would be fierce."

Ismar growled, low and deep, in his throat. "Resistance we were prepared for Kade. What we had no idea about was," he hesitated, looking for the right word, "this."

"That's the nature of unknown unknowns," said Belloc calmly.

"Oh great," said Elian, "Just great." He waved his arms about, a gesture meant to gather in the survivors from all around. "Sorry everyone, we were prepared for everything except what actually happened. What's that you say? How the shit could we be prepared for everything except what happened? Well, it appears that our competence only extends to stuff that we don't have to deal with."

"Shut up NaBaal," said Tenan. Elian whipped his head round, words already rolling off his tongue but some steady and unshakeable firmness radiated from Tenan's eyes and he found his tongue refusing to give him voice. Seeing Elian silent, Tenan nodded for Belloc to continue.

"The problems facing us are legion. Should the other Elemental Lords manage to find their arses with both hands they could descend here and now to wipe us out."

"I thought we were all convinced they wouldn't do that if we showed we could destroy them completely," said Shash. All faces focussed intently on Belloc.

"I regard the possibility as unlikely, but we're stuck hundreds of miles from our homes in the middle of a wasteland with no supplies, no army and no way of getting home. Ask yourselves what you would do if the tables were turned." To such a question there was no response.

Ismar sat forward on his crossed legs, "Setting aside these small challenges, we also have the issue we've all known about since we set ourselves on this course. The Lord of Body is dead. Properly dead."

"Likely dead," said Elian and Ismar looked as if this, of all things, might cause him to get up and beat the former Lord of Power to a pulp there and then.

"I don't know about you but my healing magic will continue to work Elian. That's not easily explained."

Tenan yawned and said, "Belloc, is there any possibility that there are other survivors?"

Belloc shook his head. "We were protected by the circle's wards. Maybe some of the wedges found a way to shield themselves in those final moments." His voice trailed off and he looked down.

"Eight legions," said Shash, feeling like he needed to throw up, as if that might clean his spirit.

"Ten," said Elian, "Don't forget that until a year ago the two legions of Instantine were also yours to command. I doubt they made it out of their beloved bread basket either."

"One hundred thousand men and women, plus those fools who didn't flee the city at our approach," said Tenan, "Such a loss is devastating. The Families have barely two legions left and should the Tuareg decide now is the right time to expand their nation we'll be overrun."

Elian snorted, "Yeah, of course, because they'll look at Instantine and think 'We definitely want some of that.'"

"I was the First amongst us," said Shash quietly.

"Does that still hold? Do you recognise me as pre-eminent still?"

Tenan laughed, his harsh short bark of humour. "Be my guest Tyan. Be my guest." The others remained quiet, only Elian looking round at each of them, his eyes measuring their fear and relief at Shash taking up his mantle of First.

"Let's count what went right," said Ismar, smoothing the tangled fronds of his moustache as it hung forlorn beneath his bulbous nose, "We have truly unmade a major Elemental Lord. Where we go from here is anyone's guess. But," he held out his hands for silence, "until now it wasn't. We have won ourselves this freedom and we should make it count."

"No one knows we won," said Belloc.

"They will," said Elian, "The Houses of Body were, like all our places of dedication, supported by his will and they will have collapsed into nothing around the time of Air this morning." Silence followed as the Firsts thought through the implications. Everyone in Akesh would know they had been successful. The Houses of Body had been closed and shuttered in the first days of the war, their followers imprisoned, executed or fled. They had been left abandoned – all the attention of the Families had been focused on Instantine and securing the major ritual circle situated in the heart of the administration's main palace.

"We need to get back then," said Tenan.

"I didn't bring my entire Family here to see some nobody decide I'm dead and take over," said Belloc. The others nodded, wondering just how long they had before they were declared dead and replaced. Not as long as they needed most likely.

Shash stood up and stretched with a loud groan. "I'll need new Hands."

"Won't we all." Muttered Elian as the others got up as well.

"Our reward from the Lords of Essence can wait. We need to get home," said Ismar. With this they returned to the oasis and started preparing for the journey home.

The next morning it was decided to return to Nabaalasan as that was the nearest of the Family cities. Tyanabad was marginally closer but the roads had been wiped away in Instantine's destruction and all agreed that as long as their direction of travel stayed true west they'd find Nabaalasan eventually. Elian considered Shash's request for recognition as First with bemusement. If the other Elemental Lords knew what was good for them they'd have left Akesh with what was left of their dignity. That they hadn't descended in the aftermath of the eradication of Instantine gave him the most perverse hope that they were rid of the meddling, power hungry demons once and for all.

Elian was missing the counsel of his second, Athanasus. His second was a good decade older than Elian and had served two firsts of NaBaal. He had been a good vizier to Elian's Shah but he had also been a good battle field advisor and was outside the circle when they had finally destroyed that decrepit and stinking husk of a bastard, the Lord of Body. It hadn't occurred to anyone that an Essence so resplendent with the joys of life and physicality would so thoroughly exterminate everything in his death throws. Just another reason that showed they had done the right thing in calling the Essence Lords' bluff and showing they could kill them if they didn't get their own way. Athanasus was never as happy with the plan as Elian, he regarded poking their tenacious and ancient allies in the eye as on a strategic par with how their ancestors had dealt with the Shab.

Elian took a different view. The Essence Lords were slowly subverting them all. Piece by piece they were taking the soul of the Kesh and replacing it with their own ambitions. To be Akesh meant to live and die as family and, as the people of Instantine had shown all of creation, they were prepared to do whatever was necessary to hold onto what made them Akesh.

Elian was brought out of his reverie by the approach of Belloc. Around them the newly minted seconds of the Families were overseeing the breaking of camp, the securing of what water they could carry with them and were tending to those newly dead members who were judged to have been too frail to make the journey home. Another sixty one to add to the total loss of life.

"Better them than all of us. They understood that," said Belloc, reading Elian's face.

Elian shrugged his agreement. "Nazari Belloc, will you walk with me today?"

Belloc made a shallow bow, an impressive feat for a man of his girth, "Negaran Elian. If you would have me."

Elian shrugged again and tried to cover his legs from the sun. His robes were ripped and torn and the chance of protecting his calves from another day of merciless heat seemed remote. The mud he had seen the others caking their exposed flesh in would crack and crumble away before the time of Fire even began.

The two men walked together at the front of the column of refugees. The other three Firsts clumped together some way back, cajoling and encouraging as required. Ismar was better at triage than Elian and the former Lord of Power found himself glad Ismar was so pleased to provide the service to the rest of them. The only price seemed to be Ismar's satisfaction that none of them had the stomach for killing the tired and weary.

"We have other problems," said Belloc.

"Do tell," said Elian, hearing some tone of concern in Belloc's voice he didn't much like.

"The Essence Lords have not descended on us. We have won that much. Yet where are they? What are they doing?"

"We don't know what impact our actions may have had on them," said Elian.

"Indeed," said Belloc, "yet they have shown themselves robust creatures, ambitious and completely alien to us. Their desire to rule, to twist and corrupt drives them Elian. So the question remains. Where are they?"

"It is possible they have gone ahead of us. It is possible they have kept forces hidden from our sight to bring our lands low in our absence. Are you suggesting they are, even now, crushing the Families while we languish in the desert choosing who is slowing us down too much to keep living?"

Belloc said nothing and the sun rose in the sky as they walked in silence. Everyone was wearing veils, to protect their faces from the sun but also to protect their lungs from the dust. They had woken that morning to find the sky clear and azure. The dust had stopped falling. Instead, as they each emerged from what shelter they had erected, they saw, for as far as they could perceive, that the land had been buried in a coating of gritty flakes of dust. The fertile farmlands of their home had been buried beneath the wreckage of the great city of Instantine; gateway to Tuareg and bread basket of Akesh.

One of Ismar's guards had claimed the dust had flecks of skin in it; bloody scabs and fingernails. None of the firsts felt the need to correct him and within the hour it was clear the veils wouldn't be coming off until they got home.

"I don't believe that," said Belloc after an eternity. "They know we have what we need to kill the rest of them. They know we could have done it at Instantine."

"I was thinking of calling that place Abadan," said Elian suddenly.

Belloc turned his head, just enough to look sidelong at Elian. "Seems fitting NaBaal."

"Don't call me that," said Elian.

"Don't be foolish NaBaal. We cannot abandon the ways of our Families just because we have finally forced the situation into the open."

"Then what Kade?" said Elian bitterly.

"We have opened the skies to our will. We must now force the issue. We must now finish this or, given time, our foe will gather themselves and strike back. I would that no more of our people die for their freedom."

Elian felt like laughing but all he could manage was a thin smile. "That is only one reason," He said. "Let me add the other two." Belloc nodded his assent. "We can subdue the Lords of Essence now. They have seen what we will do for the sake of our freedom. We can show the Families we won, that the betrayer, that fetid bag of rotting testicles, the Lord of Body, was defeated *by* the Lords of Essence and it was our cunning that saved them."

It was Belloc's turn to laugh. "Audacious NaBaal. Worthy of a First."

"We have our three reasons," said Elian.

"I shall tell the others. Shash first of course," said Belloc.

Elian knew Belloc had already been to Shash, had already discussed what they had to do with him. He was pleased enough that Belloc remembered who Elian was that he was only second in the list of Firsts. To Belloc he said nothing.

"I will support your idea Belloc. When the time comes. You should speak with Tenan next."

Belloc said nothing but turned away from Elian and dropped back into the body of the survivors. Elian watched him go and found himself watching the Ghulkan carrying the huge amphora to stored most of their water. Tough buggers and thank the Families they'd taken so many into the circle with them. The fighting inside the circle had been vicious, but more importantly, without them here, now, the rest of the survivors had no hope of carrying the water they needed to get them home. Maybe the Essence of Luck didn't hate them so completely as he'd imagined.

Shash's remaining followers had been scouting. They made their major forays at the time of Water and into the time of Earth. Returning to him they made their offerings and reported on what they'd found. In most cases what they'd found amounted to a pile of human dust. Remains of shattered farms and small towns along parched river beds. Yet more than one came back with tales that began to worry him. He was confident of his men, even after Instantine, and their stories of upside down trees, beetles the size of a man's head and spells misfiring just quickened his conviction that they'd damned themselves to be rid of creatures they didn't even understand. Still, he was more certain than the other firsts that they'd make it out of this barren wilderness.

No, what really worried him were two reports that although similar were about very different things. The first had been delivered by a young looking Shab scout called Alethariamna.

She was probably older than his grandfather and had been scouting for longer than he was alive. Rubbing the dust away from his veil as he listened to her, she reported that they were being tracked by a band of Ghulka to the north who, although they hadn't moved to intercept them, were keeping time and headed the same way. She suggested they knew the survivors were here but couldn't offer any explanation of why they hadn't approached. After swearing her to silence Shash dismissed her and when another scout came in, a dirty great Ghulka named Rackh who was peeling like he was a snake shedding his skin was ready to assume he was giving him old news.

He was wrong. Rackh had fallen behind the refugees and tracked back along the way they had come. He was breathless with anger, dismay and fear upon finding a small group, perhaps fifty or so, following in their wake. He had not engaged them but approached near enough to see they were followers of the Lord of Body.

Shash couldn't fathom how they were alive but he bade Rackh find a dozen men he trusted and report back in the morning. He was willing to stop them all to kill these bastard survivors but knew he had to make his case with the others first. Right now was not the time to act first and justify actions later. Shash drew the broken haft of his Falchata and examined its dull glint in the fading light of the day. Sighing, he realised it might take all of them to win against those in their wake and, although there were two separate groups following them, he knew in his heart the vote would choose the followers of the Lord of Body.

Tenan turned the situation on its head at the breaking of the time of Air. The five had gathered again while camp was being broken.

Shash reported back, with a parched throat, all that his scouts had found.

"There is something else," said Tenan as Shash concluded his report and requested a vote on which group to approach.

"Really?" asked Belloc, whose own cadre of spies were nothing more than a bloody memory buried beneath Instantine.

"There is a ritual circle a day's walk away. I would offer a counter proposal," said Tenan and Belloc nodded. Shash realised the two of them had already talked. Quickly looking around at Elian and Ismar it was plain Elian was also briefed. Ismar, in this as in so much else, was simply too self-absorbed to have been included.

"Perfect," said Elian.

"Why?" said Ismar, frowning as he finally worked out the others had been talking without him.

"We may have lost everything else in Abadan but our most accomplished ritualists remain. This circle is a great power, I think we're nearing what was the market of Ventakka," said Tenan. Shash felt his stomach lurch as it dawned on him what Tenan was about to propose.

"We have time before these weeping goats vulva catch us. Time enough to twist creation's arms once again." Tenan stood up and swept his hands around him, all the while keeping his eyes on Shash. "We are all too aware that we have killed the Lord of Body. Faced now with the last of his followers, we can bind them to our service."

"We retain a justification for keeping them alive, find a way to preserve healing magicks amongst our people and provide an escape route for the First amongst us should our other stratagem fail," said Elian.

Shash felt out manoeuvred and suddenly much less secure. Standing up slowly, making sure they were forced to wait until he was ready, Shash, adjusted his belts and eventually spoke. "I propose we bind these followers of the Lord of Body. I propose they become our Family of healing but we shall not permit them freedom, we shall not permit them prosperity. They shall forever be our healers but not Family. They shall forever serve us but not benefit from that service. If NaBaal's followers choose the shadows, these survivors and their descendents shall be kept at the side, forced to the edge. They shall have no city, they shall have no substance. They shall be hollowed out for our sake. We will keep them empty so we may be whole.

Ismar clapped his hands together lazily. "Fabulous. Well done all of you." He sighed theatrically before shouting, "Except there are thousands of our own Families who can heal and call on creation to knit wounds together, to stave off disease. Do not speak to me about surgery, that dullards artifice. It is no better than begging the body to do what it might anyway. I shall not consign my own flesh and blood to being hollowed out for the sake of the stories we tell ourselves."

"You will do whatever we agree Cyrenus. That is our way. We have our three justifications. What are your three reasons to object?" said Tenan.

Elian snorted, "Well the first is obviously that his brother is a healer."

Ismar ground his teeth, "What do you suggest then First?"

Shash rubbed wrung his hands and sat down unsteadily. "I am only the First. I do not rule you Ismar. What would you have us do?"

Ismar had not expected Shash to relinquish his rhetoric so readily. "I...We cannot force our healers to suffer for the foolishness of their Essence Lord. His death should not condemn them. If we wish to perpetuate the stories we tell our people about who we are then we must find a way to do as you have said," Belloc could not keep the sly snarl of victory from his face but Ismar pressed on, "We must find a way to honour their sacrifice – their willingness to give up prosperity, to be emptied out for us. We must find a way to ensure that even as we hold them at arm's length our peoples see this separation as right and honest." He was silent for a moment.

"If we don't manage this, then all our history will be shown to be a lie - when our corpses are cool and the knives of those who replaced us are clean, our names will be forgotten as Akesh crumbles into dust."

"Masterful," said Elian, who appeared to be genuinely smiling, a sight not dissimilar to a camel losing control of its bowels unexpectedly. The others nodded their agreement.

"It doesn't really matter who's following us," said Tenan.

Shash felt a huge weight lift from his shoulders, Tenan was right. They had time to prepare a ritual powerful enough to bring whoever was following them under their power but far more importantly they had found a way to make their history continue to be true. They were Akesh.

"Abadan is forgotten," said Shash, "The Kesh shall continue and our hollowed out ones will serve our bodies."

Belloc held one of his obese arms out for Ismar to grab as he struggled to climb to his feet unaided. "That's all very well," he said harshly, "but let's not forget why we're out here burning to death in the first place eh?"

# 2 THE PRICE OF AMBITION
## BY BEN HESKETH

THE COLD BLOCK sat on the table tempting him, its appearance only changing as the light from the many torches played across its surface. It's very presence a testament to his dedication and tenacity. Four years ago he had made his bargain; four years ago he had approached Halmut of Cain and made his deal.

Now he had it, the best piece of steel to come from the vaults of Cain in nine generations. He thought back over the things he had done to acquire it. From ensuring his progression to sixth of Tyan through the most duplicitous of routes, to the swords and trinkets he had made for the Cainites. Everything in his life had been bringing him to this one perfect moment, when he, Shamazad, sixth of Tyan would make the perfect knife.

He checked the forge area again. The anvil was level and positioned correctly. The water trough had been moved into place yesterday and sanctified by his friend Kamal of

Cyren to maintain a constant ice cold temperature. The bellows were new and were a gift from Mahut, a scribe of Kade. The designs attached to the wall had been approved by Laphet the seer, of the family of NaBaal.

Just one thing remained. Shamazad left the forge room.

The Hall of Tyan was hot. The pungent stench of sweat, the constant din of metal working, the flickering light were enough to distract most people, but not Shamazad. Not today. His destination clear in his mind, the route engrained in his memory, the ceremony repeated soundlessly from his lips.

The door he finally came to, of burnished bronze, fully the height of two men and the width of four, was at the centre of the Hall. The last and most important steps were in his immediate future, and so he banged upon the door three times.

Without a sound the doors opened inward, and the heat washed out. The blazing heat of an inferno, the fire from the very heart of the earth itself came licking at him.

A figure was silhouetted against the flames, as Shamazad's eyes grew accustomed to the light. A figure in full robes, with a white head dress, and a great hammer held in his two hands.

"Custodian I come to the heart of Tyan to beseech your blessing. I have an endeavour of the highest order and request the purest Heart flame to fire my forge. Only the most perfect blaze of the incandescent lord is good enough to fulfil my needs. Only the Heart of Tyan himself is pure enough, hot enough to ensure my success. Please, I ask of you now. Grant me the Heart flame so I may carry out my work."

"You're request is a strange one. Even in your position it is different that you ask for the Heart flame itself. Is not the fire that burns forever in the Hall enough?" replied the Custodian.

"I have secured the purest steel from Cainen, sought favour with Kade and Cyrenus. Consulted with NaBaal. In these things I have sought the purity of the other Essence lords. It is with the Heart flame of our lord Tyan that the final joy of creation can be achieved. Grant it to me now so I can fill my work with the strength of the Heart flame."

"Your justifications are good. You may have the Heart flame." The Custodian walked across the room and retrieved a brass cylinder from the wall, and with unhurried ease plunged his hands into the inferno above the pit at the rooms centre.

For a brief moment, Shamazad thought he detected the smell of burning and the screams of pain, but in the next the Custodian walked toward him, holding the cylinder ahead of him.

"I entrust now to you the Heart flame of Tyan. Bright be your weavings with its heat."

Shamazad took the cylinder, turned and left. He walked with reverence and fear, feeling the fury he held between his palms.

Returning to the forge he locked the door, and proceeded to disrobe absentmindedly, discarding his clothes in piles all over. The only place his attention lay was upon the cylinder. He filled the forge with the best charcoal he could get in the prescribed pattern and offered a final word to Tyan.

He opened the cylinder and poured it onto the charcoal. The tiniest small flame fell through the air, like a burning teardrop. The fire that it ignited belied its small presence. The charcoal caught immediately and the room filled with an suffocating warmth almost instantly.

Shamazad pumped the bellows and watched the flames reach skyward, the charcoal turning white in the space of a breath. The heat almost unbearable he lifted the steel with the tongues and plunged it into the fire in front of him.

Then he waited.

For five whole days he worked, plunging the steel into the flame, pumping the bellows, pulling the white steel and hammering it flat, then folding it upon itself. Shamazad repeated the process over fifty times, each time staring intently at the steel, waiting for the moment that it was prepared enough so he could begin the process of shaping it.

The sixth morning brought the revelation. The steel had a hue and strength he had never assumed possible. Everything was ready. He filled the forge once more with charcoal and pumped with all his strength, giving the last of his reserves to enrage the fire once more. His plan was to shape once and once only. And he knew it would work. This is the piece that would elevate him, this is the piece that would put him on the path to being the first. This would be the greatest knife ever made in Tyan's name.

He took a drink from the water jug on the desk, put the steel block into the fire one last time and sat to await the heating.

The crashing noise of the door smashing in awoke

Shamazad. The room was pitch black, the silence from the forge deafening. He knew he had failed.

"Shamazad, sixth of Tyan, you have failed in your endeavour! You were entrusted with the Heart flame and you let it extinguish! You are cast out of the family and your life forfeit!" The Custodian had barely raised his voice but the tone was very evident. The fire was alive in his eyes and those of his partners, and the wood splinters falling from the head of his hammer, the only things giving voice to his anger.

They grabbed Shamazad and bundled him out of the door, his head held in shame. His footsteps seeming to fall into rhythm with the sound of the thousand gongs that had started to sound out. His journey was flanked on either side by those who he once considered family, brothers and sisters in Tyan's service. They now turned their backs and fell into step behind him. The procession of several thousand head to the Heart of the Hall.

This time the brass doors were already open, all of the Custodians stood in front of it, a procession of hatred. The hammers held high forming an arch to walk through. Shamazad stumbled forward, one thought trickling from his mouth.

"Mercy! I only ever wished to serve! Have mercy upo..."

His plea was silenced by the hammer that smashed his jaw, the next his arm. The processional beat him with hammers, the insult done to the Custodians to allow the fire to go out was too much to forgive for them. They beat Shamazad one at a time; one hit at a time and never once hit his legs. He would be allowed to walk forward into the

Heart flame.

By the time he passed through the doorway he was deaf, his face smashed to a pulp, his ribs broken, his arms destroyed yet his eyes still saw the fire ahead of him, and the release it offered.

The doors closed without a sound behind him and his scream was never heard.

Later that night 3 people sat together in a spacious room. The first a tall man spoke with a voice that knew authority

"You did well. I'm pleased"

"He never even knew we were there," replied the second, her voice a distinctly female one. "We put the water jug on the table and left. He was so intent on what he was doing we could have stood there for days and he would never have noticed"

"Sister, he would never have noticed us no matter what he did," the third figure said as it sat down.

The first spoke again, whilst tossing the remains of the steel from hand to hand. "Your arrogance is unnecessary. Please do not do it again. You have done well for me this time. Now leave me it is far past time I slept, and I have the plans for a new knife to study tomorrow"

# 3 MOTHER
## BY ANDY COOK

"Sshhh," she gently whispered into the darkness.

She scanned her surroundings intently as she held her sister's body close. "I am so sorry Velin, I always held you dear but I had no choice, it's all for him now, there can be no us anymore." She brushed the hair from Velin's face and laid the now still frame on the ground, carefully removing her slim blade from the body; she wiped the tears from Velin's cold eyes and moved off into the darkness.

Breath held, she quietly pushed open the front door to the small squat house and stealthily moved into the room beyond. The building was of simple design, being only two rooms over one story, synonymous with many of the small desert communities scattered across Akesh. Once she was sure it was safe, she sat and in what felt like the first time in an age, her defences crumbled and her body shook.

"How had it come to this?" she thought as she looked down at the blood staining her hands," After everything we had been through together, everything we dreamed of together, being with him together." She fought back the tears and her mind fled back to three days earlier.

She heard the door open and looked up from her work; Velin entered the room with a broad smile splitting her delicate features. She always found it odd that even though she and Velin had emerged from their mother but minutes apart, that was where the similarities ended. Velin was full of life with a ready smile, always eager to help whether by word or gesture, Velin excelled at her lessons absorbing all of the knowledge given to her. Even the hollow ones praised her constantly and more often than not they would call for Velin to warm their beds on a cold night. She sighed and put down her quill.

"We have been summoned to the Great Hall." Velin excitedly told her sister.

"What for? By whom?"

"I am not sure why but Matron Dash has ordered that we are all to attend immediately and in full uniform," replied Velin, strapping her sword to her waist. "Come on hurry up or we will both be late and in serious trouble." With that she hurried out the door, leaving her sister reaching for her slim daggers, desperately trying to catch up.

They hurried through the long cold corridors, worn by the comings and goings of many would be Hands before them, all of them with the same singular thought, the same overriding, all-consuming goal; to become a Hand to the First of all Akesh, The Ascendant. To become their lover, their advisor, their protector, to carry out any duty the Ascendant wished to the best of her ability, without hesitation, without question, without remorse. Although many had carried such dreams, precious few had realised them.

As they approached the Great Hall they could hear the low hum of whispered conversation. Although the sisters had been there many times before, the magnificence of the Great Hall still made them catch their breath. The vaulted ceiling towered over their heads, with small carved openings to the sky so that the rain and wind might be felt, in deference to both Kade and Cyrenus. A massive fire blazed in the north wall opposite them, some fifty feet away, kept safe behind a large wrought iron grate fashioned into the symbol of Tyan, while the floor had not a tile laid but, in honour of Cainan, was left as naked earth, packed hard by years of use. Sigils adorned the east and west walls and many had speculated that the followers of NaBaal were their creators, for, if you stood close enough, you could feel the power emanating from them but, as is the way of NaBaal, no one could say for certain whether they'd had a hand in the creation of these strange devices or not.

The sisters entered the hall, feeling the heat of the great fire almost immediately. Looking about it seemed to them that all of the other students were here as well, spread out and huddled in small groups quietly discussing why they had all been summoned. Velin moved across the hard earth and sat with three others, gratefully accepting a sheesha pipe handed to her and falling easily in to the conversation; no one knew why they had been called together neither could they guess. Velin looked up and could see her sister standing awkwardly on her own, seemingly unable or maybe unwilling to engage anyone in the hall. Velin smiled, rose and gently encouraged her to join them.

Matron Dash swept in to the hall, the head of the order, dressed in her customary black and grey, the only sound now was the popping and cracking of the huge fire. She walked to the far end of the hall and turned to face those assembled. Standing in front of the fire her small figure seemed to be wreathed in flame, her hard, uncaring face taking on a demonic visage. The matron spoke, her words ringing out, filling the entire hall with her soft yet commanding tones, a voice in stark contrast to her stern countenance.

"Ladies, we have a guest who has journeyed all the way from Cyren to address you all, Listen to his words well; as all that you are and all that you could be will depend on it"

From the doorway a measured and considered voice spoke, "Thank you Matron Dash and you are quite correct for what I am about to say will change your lives profoundly and completely."

All eyes turned towards the speaker and they saw, striding towards the centre of the hall, a tall man, just over 6 feet in height, dressed in the drab green and browns of the Hollow ones. Although obviously a little too fond of good food and drink, he carried himself confidently and with surprising grace for a man of his size. Once he had his place in the great hall he paused, found his centre, raised his head and continued in his address, few being able to hold his intense gaze.

"The Five have come to a decision, a decision almost as profound as the bargains stuck so many years ago. It has been decided that a force from Akesh will sail across the great sea, seeking the continent to the east and five of you will have an important role to play." The Hollow One paused momentarily in his delivery to let his words sink in, delighting in the expressions of uncertainty on the faces of his audience. Once satisfied he continued. "The leadership of this expedition will fall to the Five, not the Five that looks over us now, no, but a newly wrought Five, brought together by the wisdom of those that look over us all." The speaker stopped to scrutinize his audience, disgruntled that there seemed to be no reaction, he quickly continued. "This means a new Ascendant and an Ascendant requires Hands." Now he received the reaction he was expecting; he was pleased. He allowed the commotion to continue for a few moments then raised his voice and spoke with such passion and authority that the room was stilled and all turned their gaze to him. "I will be returning to Cyren within the week and five of you will accompany me. With the help of Matron Dash I will be deciding those who are to travel with me, over the next four days you will be tested to your very limits. You are to return here at first light tomorrow, bring what you think you will need and we will begin the cull." With that the hollow one smiled a vicious smile, turned and headed towards the door leaving a stunned silence behind him.

Velin turned her head slowly, looking directly in to her sister's wide, incredulous eyes, she searched her mind for the correct words to say to her "By Tyan's balls, who was that?" was all she could muster.

A soft voice behind Velin made her jump "That, my dear, will be the Voice of the Hollow ones in the new world; if I was you I would heed his words well and turn your thoughts to your immediate future." She turned and saw a darker skinned man, she had not noticed before, she made to answer him but he had already turned and started to the follow The Voice out of the door, leaving Velin only able to wonder at his words and marvel at his large purple collar.

The next two days were filled with many lessons and trials, The Voice proved to be a relentless taskmaster; allowing no rest and demanding complete and total obedience. Sleep and relaxation proved to be a commodity in very short supply and the would-be-Hands were pushed to their very limits. Velin would never be sure what caused the 'incident' to happen but she could only put it down to the strain of the last two days. They had all been summoned at the end of the second day, by The Voice, to assemble in the great hall. It was getting late and the would-be-Hands, weary beyond words, sat around hall in silence enjoying the rest and a pipe. The Voice entered and walked to the middle of the hall and looked around him, he spoke, his voice carrying a dangerous edge.

"I enter the room and you still sit!" he quietly spoke. "Is this how you will behave when you serve the Ascendant?" he looked around the room and all were pulling themselves to their feet apart from one who sat in defiance of his words. The Voice moved to sit beside the recalcitrant student. "Remind me of your name," the voice asked as he sat down next to her.

"I am Tashin," she responded with defiant tones.

"Why do you defy me Tashin?" asked The Voice. "I told you when we started that I expect your obedience during the selection process"

"This is not a selection process," spat Tashin, "This

is just a way for you to warm your bed at night and take out your annoyance at the world on us, I will serve Him not you, I am not yours to command I am His." Tashin locked eyes with the Voice and did not look away, all she could hear was her heart pounding in her chest as utter silence filled the hall.

The Voice smiled and reclined onto the cushions, "I like your fire Tashin I really do," he chuckled as he reached for a pipe. "It may serve you well when you serve the Ascendant" Tashin visibly relaxed and smiled.

"Thank you Voice, I am glad you recognise my talents," she said as she laid back on to the cushion her voice softer but still with an edge.

"Oh, I recognise your talents Tashin," Voice said never taking his gaze form hers. "I also recognise your arrogance which I cannot allow." With that he spoke quietly under his breath and reached his hand out towards her chest. Tashin realised her fate too late, she felt his palm upon her breast, felt the surge of power rip through her body, then she knew no more. The hollow one stood and addressed the stunned and shaken audience "You may rest tomorrow; gather here the following day for your final assessment." With that he left.

It was a bright day that followed 'the incident' and Velin sat with her sister in the grounds. "I am so excited about serving him, I can think of nothing else," said Velin. "We have both done so well we are bound to be chosen." Her sister just smiled in response but still sharing in her excitement. They sat then, talking for hours about their plans, how they would make sure they are selected and what it will be like to serve him. As time drew on and darkness descended Velin became tired but her sister was wakeful, she wished to enjoy the night air and clear her mind ready for tomorrow, so Velin stood, kissed her sister gently and lovingly on the forehead and left for her bed.

As the night drew on the air became chill, so she made her way back to her sleeping quarters, thinking on her sister's words and smiling to herself about how much the Ascendant would enjoy Velin's company. As she walked past the doors to the great hall she heard voices' coming from within, it was late so she stopped, intrigued to know who was still up at this hour. Carefully peeking around the doorway she saw The Voice standing with his back to her, speaking to Matron Dash who took her ease amongst the floor cushions.

"What about the twins?" Matron Dash asked looking up at the Hollow One above her.

"Hhhmm a tricky one indeed." The hollow one replied thoughtfully. "I am not sure what to do about it."

"They both deserve to go through on the morning's selection Voice" Dash said, quickly.

"Yes, yes Dash I agree with your point on the selection but I question their loyalty." The Hollow one held up his hand quickly heading off the Matrons protestations. "The bond they share is hard to break; I do not believe for a moment that they would cause a threat to the Ascendant in fact I believe that they would both give everything they are for him but…." The Hollow one paused and gathered his thoughts for a time and then continued, "It concerns me that this could become a conflict of issues at a crucial point, this could cause I am sure you would agree, an issue with regards to the safety of the Ascendant."

"Yes I agree but what exactly are you trying to suggest Voice" the Matron asked, not seeming to follow The Hollow ones train of thought.

"I am saying Matron that I may select both of them tomorrow but only *one* of them may make it to the Ascendants side."

"How do you think that will happen Voice," the Matron replied in an amused and slightly dismissive tone. "They were practically inseparable before you arrived; their bond is as stone now. It will not be as easy as you seem to think it will be."

"Oh, I do not know Matron, I think the bond maybe weaker than you think," in saying, he turned and looked directly at the empty doorway behind him, a sad expression spread across his face as he continued "Do not worry though Matron, I have a feeling everything will sort itself out."

There was a feeling of excitement in the great hall, Tashin long forgotten, the selection the only thought on anyone's mind. Velin looked for her sister and saw her standing, gazing in to the fire, alone.

"Come on, sister." Velin took her twin's hand to guide her back into the excited throng but it was resisted. "What is wrong? Is your mind not whirling with the possibilities of what we could achieve if we are chosen?" Velin looked more closely at her sister's face "Why so sad? You look pale, are you ill?" Velin asked now very concerned for her sister's health.

"Yes, my dearest sister I have thought of nothing

else since I returned to sleep." She took Velin's hand in hers, kissed it tenderly and without letting go turned back to stare into the fire. Velin unsure of her sister's sadness hugged her close and reassured her nothing could or would ever separate them.

The Voice and Matron Dash entered, everyone immediately stood. The Voice looked about him taking in all the faces waiting for him to decide their fate, waiting for him to decide if they were good enough to serve the Ascendant. He drew himself up and spoke.

"I have made a decision on who will be selected. At first I was hoping to only chose five of you but that is not the case I have chosen fifteen of you." With this, the would-be-Hands strayed from their normal discipline and broke in to heated discussions with each other. "BE SILENT!" The hollow one bellowed. "Listen to my words or things will be all the worse for you," he waited for the room to quieten and then continued. "I will point to you, this will mean you have been chosen, go and collected your possessions and wait for me at the front entrance, we leave form the ports of Cyren Immediately." The Hollow One looked around the room pointing out the ones he wished to travel with him and one by one they left to collect their belongings. Velin, still hand in hand with her sister, become worried as others were chosen over her and her sister, then the Hollow One turned his gaze to them. He studied them both for what seemed like, to Velin, an age, his face as cold as stone giving away no emotion, with a nod of his head he finally seemed to reach a decision. "You both will go."

The fifteen chosen stood uncertainly outside in the already warm sun, they were all dressed in the black and grey of the Hands uniform, bedecked in weapons and travelling attire. The Voice appeared from the courtyard astride his camel, another five tied in line behind him. "We have a ways to go so we will waste no time" with that he dug his feet into the sides of his mount leaving the Hands to catch up. They travelled for the rest of the day, only stopping once to take on food and water, when as darkness fell they came across an abandoned village and The Voice reigned in his camel. "We shall eat and rest here," he proclaimed as he dismounted and drew forth his rations and a small pipe. The Hands settled down to a routine, some scavenged fire wood while others set the camp after this was all done they finally ate. It was approaching midnight when The Voice rose and spoke to his charges.

"Hands, as you know I will only take five of you across the sea to serve the Ascendant and I have been trying to come up with a way to decide which ones of you to take, You all have the ability to serve, you all have the will to serve, you all have the need to serve. " The first amongst the hollow ones paused as if deep in thought and stared into the fire for a while, then he looked up from the flames, his face once again as hard as iron, as cold as the snow from the highest mountains and he spoke, in a dreadful low whisper. "So I have decided to leave it down to you, I will meet the Five of you that make it in the docks of Cyren." The Hollow mounted his camel and turned loose the five camels tied to his saddle and without another word he turned into the darkness and rode off.

For the merest moment there was no movement, not a sound other than wind whistling through the broken windows of the abandoned village then the camp exploded into motion. The hands grabbed what they could and scattered into the darkness, Velin grabbed her sword knowing without looking that her sister was scant seconds behind her and barrelled in to the darkness, into the village to seek refuge in one of the many disused houses. Velin reached the door and looked around for her sister to beckon her inside so that they may plan next move, the allies they would need to gather. As she turned to speak with her sister, Velin was startled to see her standing almost directly behind her. For that moment time seemed to slow, the twins just stood, staring at each other, no sound just her sister's face, Velin confused, made to speak, an explosion of pain, she looked down, the flash of cold hard steel, time crashed in, legs gave way and she fell. Velin lay in her sister's arms, she stared quietly up into the eyes of the only person that she had truly cared for, the only one she had truly loved. "Why?" was her last word.

The snap of a branch jolted her suddenly and violently back to the present, someone was outside. She wiped the blood away from her hands on to her already stained clothing and gathered her weapons to her. As quietly as the falling snow she made her way to the door, listened intently and on hearing nothing opened it ever so slightly. She saw her sister's body lying on the cold hard earth another Hand stripping the corpse of it possessions, unable to tell who it was, as their back was towards her, she closed the door to gather her thoughts.

"How dare she?" she thought angrily "how dare she? Has she no respect?" Her anger grew as she peered around the door to see the Hand going through Velin's discarded pack. "You, my corpse robbing friend, will pay for disrespect with your life" she slid quietly through the gap in the door, daggers making no sound as they were drawn from their sheath, breath held, she closed within striking distance......

She heard no sound before the white hot agony surged through her body, confusion gripped her, what had happened? She tried to turn and raise her weapons in defence but her body would not conform to her will, she looked down and saw the tip of a dagger tear through the front of the black and grey she held so dear, fear, all-consuming fear stripped away her logical mind. She fell backwards, her legs no longer able to bear her weight, and was caught before she hit the ground, she stared into the face of her killer, her assassin, her murderer but all she could see was large, almond shaped, brown eyes staring unblinking down at her. As the stark terror welled up inside her she tried to scream, no sound came forth but she did see bright red flecks appear around the edges of those large staring eyes.

"MOTHER HELP ME" she silently screamed, fear, a cold unbridled fear, then blackness

"MOTHER PLEASE DON'T LEAVE ME" hot tears on a cold cheek, panic, then blackness

"MOTHER...... I'm sorry" a strange calm, acceptance, then nothing.

"I never liked you much Valin," said brown eyes as she dropped the body to the floor, "we could certainly not let you serve Him after you killed Velin, you have no idea what it means to be a Hand," with that the young woman with brown eyes nodded to her sister crouching over Velin's body and moved away to join the other three as they emerged from the darkness, either not seeing or not caring about the tears in Valin's cold, unseeing eyes.

# 4 THE JUSTIFICATIONS
## BY STEWART HOTSTON

The man was dead. Sael closed his eyes with the tips of her fingers but didn't stand up straight away. There were twenty people in the room watching her heal the man on the orders of Cainen's second. Of course, Cainen's second meant kill when he said heal but that was the contract; Sael would let Aelish worry about his own justification.

The dead man was a Cainenite brewer by the name of Keb, although the clerk hovering at the back of the room had assured her the man was a Face for a coven. Aelish had denied the nature of the coven's research was the crime but Sael had to wonder if that was the Cainenite being entirely honest.

Keb had been far from dead when Sael arrived. The alchemist had been stabbed in the chest, once, but Sael had seen her fair share of battlefields and such wounds were no more serious for someone with her talent than a torn fingernail. Healing is all about timing. Arrive to early, and well, you should have stayed in that nice, warm and very expensive bath a family had paid for in gratitude for your saving of their only son. Arrive too late? Same story really.

Aelish, and the clerk, whose name she didn't know, had individually informed her that Keb was guilty of breaking the law and deserved to die.

Normally she would have held authority in a case like this. Sael's other main duty, especially in peace time, was to act as a wandering judge. She loved the sea, so had found herself a circuit that took her along the western edge of Akesh for most of the year before returning her to Kadabad around New Year. There weren't many large towns once one left the Kad peninsula and meandered west into the last scraps of Akesh's mainland forests but there were many small settlements. Farms, lumber villages, Shab hamlets in the deep wilds. They were too small for most of the luxuries of civilisation like running water, markets or Houses of the Five and she fulfilled an essential role – that of arbitrator.

Sael was Hollow. She was a servant of the Kesh. She was trusted to hold to the ideal of everything that the Families stood for; starting with loyalty to the Families. Normally, at this point, Keb would still have been alive until she decided his guilt. However, for some unknown reason, a Second of Cainen was also a guest in the lumber mill and its surrounding village. He was a voice of the Kesh, not simply its servant, and as with everyone else she had to listen when the voices of the Kesh spoke.

"Get me the Order," said Aelish, and several people ran from the large tent where the execution had been carried out.

Sael straightened up and began to make her way out. She was desperate to avoid becoming embroiled in the politics of the judgement. Even if Aelish was the most powerful man in the settlement, the fourth of Tyan who actually ran the mill could still challenge his decision. Elements Abandon them, anyone could challenge the decision, even in retrospect, but none would dare stand up to a second without some serious sense of entitlement if they didn't also want to share the fate of the condemned. As it stood, an adherent of NaBaal, a Second of Cainen and a Hollow One had all declared, in their actions if not just their words, the accused to be guilty of his crime.

Except I don't know what he even did, thought Sael, just as she reached the entrance to the tent.

"Honoured Hollow One," called out Aelish. Sael cursed her bad luck but stopped herself from leaving. Hood up and face hidden as she was prepared to go outside she waited.

"I would have you stay until the Order of Path and Place have their task."

"Very well," announced Sael, for her own benefit. She had to maintain the sense that she was this Second's peer amongst these, her constituents. Turning back to face the room she saw the clerk motioning for her to sit near him. She sighed; just crossing the room left her snared in the politics of the whole shit show. Worse still, she could smell the fetid stench of self interest coming off Aelish in clouds. Whatever happened to Aelish, and she had no reason to doubt his actions other than the turn of her stomach when she saw his face, the people who lived here would see her as someone else's tool. She had spent years helping them, looking out for them and defending them from each other and in as simple an action as doing nothing she may have damaged that trust irreparably.

It was the Time of Water before the nearest member of the Order could be found and brought to the settlement. Ish was the Ghulkorg leader of the small family who patrolled the wilds on behalf of those who traversed and worked the far interior. Even the Shab, who practically walked without leaving footprints in wet sand, respected their knowledge of the wild places of Akesh. Most Kesh thought the Order of Path and Place tended the desolate lands surrounding Abadan. For the most part this was true, they had begun there and still found much of their purpose in maintaining those small oases and secret paths that allowed successful navigation of the great desert in the very heart of Akesh.

However, Akesh had other wild places and, in the decades following their blessing by the Five, after having brought them safely from the wreckage of Abadan following the defeat of the Lord of Body on behalf of the true Lords of Essence, they had found other places the Families were thankful for them to be.

Ish was a Terraka, one of those giants of the Ghulka. Eight foot tall, he had long hairy slicked back ears of which he was particularly proud. His tusks weren't ever going to win him the choice of any females he might want but then the females who ruled the men with long tusks were just a bit too demanding for his tastes. He was happiest out in the wilds, far away from the cities of the Terraka and the Kesh. Amongst the Order of Path and Place he was known as

Bark because of his soft skin and clear complexion – something other members of the Order found a source of amusement. Since most of the community were desert dwellers their faces really were gnarled, cracked and tough as old boots.

He had been busy repairing a rope bridge across a shallow gorge about three miles from the settlement. It wasn't an important route but Ish knew that carelessness about the small things would lead to disaster at just the moment when one needed them to take care of themselves.

All the messenger had told him was that someone had been found guilty of crimes against the Kesh. The young Kesh didn't need to say more; Ish knew what that meant. There was something to be said for the Kesh – they didn't tolerate disloyalty or weakness and Ish admired a people who, although so physically small, were so ferociously committed to such virtuous ideals. Bemused that they would call on him over such a matter he finished weaving the guide rope back into the post where it had frayed away and then secured it using a bone and metal pin. Once he was satisfied with his work he sent the , by now desperately bored, young man on to find his family and let them know they were needed. They were spread out across the wilds tending small patches of the last forests, but all would come to join him before the next time of Air.

Ish could smell something wrong as he jogged into camp; it was quiet and the entire lumber plant had stopped working. The normal buzz of people running around, busy at their work, was missing. There weren't even any people milling around doing bugger all except gossiping.

The settlement itself was composed of a number of

larger canvas tents, some as large as sixty feet per span with two or three spans. All the Families of Kesh had space here and Ish had counted a hundred or so Kesh households along with splinters of three different Ghulka tribes. The local population probably numbered around three hundred people and that didn't include traders and the more transient work force who came and went with the lumber caravans which took the felled wood inland.

Ish and his kin didn't just maintain the paths through the forests, they policed them. There were always disloyal folk who thought they could turn a quick profit from felling the few remaining trees against the interest of the Kesh. The Order spent its time here, when not repairing and tending routes, tracking and spotting disloyal loggers.

"Who are you?" demanded a skinny Kesh as Ish bent to come into the tent where most of the settlement seemed to be gathered. Ish wasn't used to being asked and assumed it was an outsider. Letting his eyes adjust to the gloom he looked the Kesh up and down and judged what he saw. The Kesh's eyes were firm and clear, his hands callused and used. His clothing was of a high quality but not ornate and he wore the symbol of Cainen on his overcoat. It was enough for Ish to know he should show respect rather than batter the man around the head for his rudeness.

"I am of the Order," said Ish. Now he was here he noted the corpse being prepared for a Cainenite death near the entrance he had entered through. A number of people were wrapping him carefully in a pale taupe gauze before he would be taken somewhere secret and buried beneath the ground.

Ish had to stop his mouth from watering.

A Hollow One stood further back, near an Essence damned clerk if Ish was any judge. Sighing inwardly, he began to form an idea of what was happening around him.

The Second moved forward, walking without regard for those around him and, sure enough, they stepped back to make way. He didn't come all the way to Ish, which Ish supposed was because he towered over the Kesh and it wouldn't give the right impression.

"The judged was consorting with the disloyal and the enemies of the Akesh." The Second looked around the room, ensuring everyone knew he was speaking to them. "I have summoned the Order of Path and Place because he was not alone."

Ah crap, thought Ish.

The Second then dismissed the people in the hall.

When the space had been cleared, Ish found himself with the two remaining members of the dead man's coven together with the clerk and the Hollow One.

The Cainenite introduced himself, "I am Aelish, Fifth Second of Cainen. You should know what you're looking for."

Ish looked at the coven members. A man and a woman, unrelated, although it could be difficult to tell with Kesh, they didn't have any of the features he considered remarkable and distinctive in his own kind. They weren't bound, but the look on their faces indicated their day wasn't over yet. That they weren't dead meant they would probably leave on their feet, but they had been weak enough to be fooled by a betrayer and he assumed they'd be out on their ears in less than a cycle of the moon. Their families would be shamed as much by their surviving than by any actual execution.

"What is it I seek?" asked Ish.

Aelish sat himself down on a low bench by the washing bowl at the nearest entrance.

"You are looking for a small group of former Kesh. They have all been found guilty of betraying the Families." Ish noticed the clerk raise an eyebrow, "They will likely be armed and have headed north. Although a long journey, it is likely their destination are the mountains north of Cyren."

"Why would they head there?" asked Ish, feeling heat prickle his skin at the mention of the Kesh city nearest his home.

"That is not your business," said Aelish.

"It is my calling to find these betrayers. Second, you must give me what I need if I am to be successful. Second, you must give me what I request so I am prepared. Second, you must give me what I request so I understand their motives."

Aelish sat in silence, his eyes reflecting the glint of the water in the bowl beside him. Eventually he spoke, "Very well, I accept your justification. There is reason to believe the betrayers are in the service of a Ghulkak."

Ish gasped, "Don't pull my tusks."

Aelish scowled, "I am not."

Ish's heart was already racing and, ducking to get clearance from the lintel over the exit, he said "I shall leave now Second."

"You've the brain of a puss filled boil Aelish," said the clerk.

Sael looked at the two of them and wondered what

in Tyan's name was going on.

"That may be true," said Aelish and turned to the two coven members, "you two, explain to me why you were working with Keb."

The two of them looked at each other and the woman spoke. She was of an indeterminate age, somewhere between thirty and fifty years old. The gentle weather here, and her own occupation, ensured it was hard for Sael to pinpoint how old she was.

"We've been together as a coven for twelve years Second. We never suspected." Her voice trailed off. Good decision, thought Sael.

"That's why I haven't judged you as severely," said Aelish, "but so we're clear, he was using alchemy to influence people's spirits. As you know this is an insult against the Essence Lords themselves."

Aelish waited for them to speak but they said nothing. Sael watched a range of emotions pass across his face and was keenly aware of how the alchemists responded to each new expression he pulled. However, they did not venture anything more.

After several minutes of silence Aelish said, "have you nothing to say for yourselves?"

"I doubt they know what to say," said the clerk, his tone of voice so dry it felt like a desert wind had swept in from across the foothills to the east.

"And why's that?" asked Aelish out of the corner of his mouth.

Sael sighed as the clerk said, "Because, you great turd, alchemy can never, ever, work in conjunction with the pure exercise of an Essence Lord's will."

"I'm tiring of your challenges," said Aelish thickly and he turned to the clerk who, in turn, held the Cainenite's gaze without wavering.

"I'm tiring of having to point out your incompetence Aelish. At least it appears like incompetence to me," said the clerk flatly. Aelish turned away and looked at the coven members.

"Tell me why you were committing disloyalty by attempting to influence people's spirits," he said again.

"Aelish," said the clerk firmly this time.

"Silence. I will have your observance but not your interference; unless you can find a justification for challenging my decision," shrieked Aelish. The Second waited a moment, and nodded to himself before turning back to his prisoners. The clerk watched them, but said nothing more.

Sael was thinking as fast as her mind would allow. She had no head for politics and had always avoided taking sides. The beauty of her role as judge was that it allowed her to be impartial. Yet here was a man in power demonstrating bias, incompetence and who was hiding his true intentions from those who he should have been open with. Her stomach turned over as she tried to find a route through.

The female prisoner, wringing her hands as she spoke, said "Second, the clerk is right, what you say cannot be done." Her eyes clung desperately to him.

"So you say," said Aelish, not looking around at the clerk. Sael felt as she had been forgotten.

"It's true," said the accused woman.

The clerk stood up and folded his arms across his chest. "You've splendidly screwed this up. Better a poisonous oyster than any more of your plans."

Aelish forgot his prey and whipped around to face the clerk. "So you'll challenge me then?" he said furiously.

The clerk shook his head, "No. You may have doomed that Ghulkorg to death at the hands of your own men, you may have lost a Ghulkak we've been tracking for three years and you may have not even the most basic understanding of the Elements but I shall not challenge you."

Aelish's body relaxed and Sael felt herself breath out with him.

"You had just better hope your men deal with the Order or I know someone who will have ample justification for challenging you," said the clerk.

Sael rose to her feet, dizzy with what she was about to do. "I challenge you," said the words which came out of her mouth.

The clerk laughed in a raggedly delighted whoop that ended in a coughing fit.

"On what grounds?" said Aelish, his eyes wide with shock at her action.

Sael knew she was his equal, that she could challenge him as a peer. She was a Hollow One, if she, as a servant of the Kesh was a challenger, only the Five themselves might be able to avoid answering her directly.

"As the clerk said." She tilted her head in his direction, "A five year old Ghulka understands more about the Elements than you."

Aelish shook his head, a nasty sneer crossing his face, "Those are not grounds," he said.

The clerk spoke, "She means that your inability to

grasp the most basic facts about the Spiritual, the Elemental and the Alchemical realms means you have accused these two here of something not remotely possible. The implication is, you are hiding something."

Sael said nothing, she was struggling to breathe.

"Very well," said Aelish, "present your case."

It took Ish half a full cycle of the elements to be confident he had found the right tracks. He had been following a poorly concealed path heading north from the settlement for a quarter cycle but something about it had been wrong. He couldn't put his finger on it but was suspicious the path wasn't the one he was looking for. The signs were clear enough that people had passed that way, Kesh and Ghulka together, but there was no rush, no changing of pace. The direction was straight as an arrow, over obstacles that people travelling a long distance would normally, unconsciously, avoid.

He cut diagonally across the path several times, looking for other, more likely, signs of passage but could find none. With a lack of alternatives and this one standing out like his wife's nipples on a cold night he eventually concluded it was where he was meant to be.

He settled into an easy lope, given the pace they were setting he would catch them in less than a day. Catching them was different to taking them on. If there was a Ghulkak amongst them he was not leaving anything to chance. He left clear signs of his passage and his intentions for his family. He would not be coming back without the Ghulkak's head.

When tracking loggers who had no justification for

their activity he would circle ahead of them and find ground that suited him. He preferred locations with higher ground. If they were fortunate enough to be in densely wooded areas, of which there were few left, he would lure them there. Ish would attack from cover and attempt to take down the most senior member of the band and offer the others a public trial

As a safeguard he would prepare simple traps with the materials at hand. Typically he chose snares and clamps that would spring shut and disable his quarry. Disloyalty should be shown in public and shamed – killing them alone in the wilds spared them the full punishment of being outcast by their Families.

More than one man had broken as his children spat on him, as his wife turned away and took her shoes off, to signify she was starting a new life, her feet resting on the naked earth which gave her birth. Men in chains still wept when all that was left around them were empty sandals and dusty echoes of the lives they had lost. Ish was only satisfied when their betrayal was truly brought home to them.

Occupying himself with the satisfaction he would find in bringing shame on this group and in a reverie of throwing the Ghulkak's dried out head at the feet of his family's First, he missed a turn in the track. Finding that he had come off the path he retraced his route until he found it again.

Looking at a broken branch he felt his unease return. This time he knew why he had been so uncertain about the trail; the path had been laid and then been deliberately concealed as if by someone who didn't care if they were followed.

He realised they had done this so he could find them. They wanted their pursuer to catch them. He skin tightened over his muscles as he realised he could rely on nothing he believed he had discerned from the trail. Numbers, composition, speed and competence were all lies sown to keep him from seeing the truth.

Ish stilled his heart, forced the rush in his stomach to fade and listened to the land around him. He could have wept as he realised the nearest bird was several metres away, that there were no mammals near the path.

Ish closed his eyes and listened with his whole body. He sniffed the air, his great nostrils taking in long, slow and measured currents from the woodland around him.

They knew he knew.

Ish smiled and loosened the great ax at his back with one arm while relaxing his body into a fighting stance. He knew they knew.

He thought through the land around him. A few trees, enough to call it woodland by Kesh standards, but still spacious enough to fight with his precious ax. The ground was flat nearby but sloped off sharply to his right about five yards away. A small rise he had passed was where he expected them to be hiding. He wasn't quite close enough for anyone to make it to him before he could turn and face them. Unless they believed he was preoccupied.

It wasn't much of an advantage but it was all he had. Ish committed himself to the Lords of Essence and knelt down on one knee. Moving one hand across the ground, as if trying to pick up information from the trail, he started talking to himself.

Almost immediately he heard dry leaves crushed behind him. He waited one, two, three heart beats before twisting on his foot, unpinning his ax with one arm and flinging his hunting knife with the other.

"Ack." Coughed one of the three Kesh charging over the rise and he fell, blood gurgling and frothing out of his mouth with Ish's knife standing proud from his chest.

Ish unlimbered his axe and stepped into the swing of the first Kesh to reach him. He was nearly two feet taller than his opponent but no less swift and his ax bit through the man's leather helmet as if it were a pig's tit. Ish stepped back and span to his right as the third of the Kesh reached him. His ax was stuck in the second man's head and using his body as a shield he flung the flailing corpse out and between them.

His enemy was over his surprise and, slipping sideways around his dead companion, showed he was competent and focussed.

Ish was not concerned. He could reach the man without putting himself in danger and the long sabre might have posed a threat to him, if all three had faced him as one, but now was about as likely to bring him low as a knitting needle.

There was a sudden searing pain across his back and stumbling forwards, just barely parrying an opportunistic jab from the man in front of him, Ish realised he was in trouble. The gash across his back was hot and bleeding freely. He could feel his life draining down into the crack between his buttocks. Moving backwards and turning he could see that another three men, followed by two Ghulka, had been waiting on the path ahead of him. They must have heard the fight break out and had come rushing down the path and attacked him from behind.

One of the Kesh had scraped his scimitar long and hard across Ish's exposed back.

Ish grew angry. He searched for the Ghulkak. He wasn't to be seen. Of course he wasn't to be seen. These bastards had known someone was following them. Had planned for it. The Ghulkak would be safely somewhere else and probably had been all along.

One of Kesh rushed forward, Ish batted him aside with the flat of the ax head and as he stamped down on the tumbling figure brought his weapon round and severed his arm. The limb wasn't cleanly sliced through and the man screamed as he tried to hold his arm to his body.

Ish stepped back; the last move had cost him and looking around he could tell the remaining soldiers knew he was weakening.

Ax held up in front of him he waited for them to charge. He reckoned he could take down maybe one more before they overwhelmed him and the thought made him curse the Cainenite who had sent him out here to die. The group slowly surrounded him, keeping their distance until they were ready to take him down. It was then he noticed a Cainenite symbol over the heart of the closest Ghulka.

Ish committed his body to the creatures of the wilds, wishing he wouldn't lie long before being devoured. As he was finishing his devotion, an unholy battle cry he recognised as a woman enraged by his stupidity changed everything; his family charged headlong down the road from the direction of the settlement. The sight of a dozen Ghulkorg charging towards them brought the soldiers up short, but before they could reform their line to meet the incoming attack, the giant mountains of steel and edges that were Ish's family ploughed into them.

They argued all through the time of earth. Aelish found himself on the back foot for most of it, but as the truth came out the Hollow One slowly backed up, refusing, at first to even believe why he and the third of NaBaal had enacted the strategy she was challenging. He respected the justifications she placed before him but as he argued his position before her, Aelish remembered why he had found himself with no other option than to take such great risks. The danger of not acting was more devastating than the life of one Ghulkorg and a single coven.

"Your justifications are acceptable but they are not sufficient," said Aelish, "The Ghulkak is real and the threat is underestimated. By sending out a single member of the Order, as I have done, the Families will wake up to the menace growing in the heart of Akesh."

The clerk sighed in resignation, a lonely and tired sound that left Sael wondering why he had countenanced her challenge in the first place.

"Yes, I have been foolish, but the Face of the coven was conspiring with agents of disloyalty. What were we to do?" asked the Second.

"Ish will be killed by your own men!" repeated Sael. It was the last of her justifications that held any weight. "You cannot sacrifice a member of the families for some supposed benefit to the rest of Akesh. It doesn't matter what the consequences."

"And would you be satisfied if he had consented?"

"He would not have died if you had told him the truth," said Sael

"The Ghulkak is real!" shouted Aelish.

"That much is true," said the clerk.

"Then prove it," said Sael emphatically.

Aelish shook his head as if she were feeble minded, "Do you have any idea what you're saying? They are cunning little bastards. We've been hunting him three years and have only seen him that first time and then once more in the sewers of Tyanabad. He has followers even among the Kesh. He was here. We know it and Keb was his contact for a potion which we know influenced people's loyalties."

Sael bit her tongue. After Aelish's outlandish claims relating to Keb's research the clerk had confirmed that the alchemist was trying to achieve an effect like that the Lords of Essence granted but without actually relying on them. Sael still doubted their story but the clerk seemed neutral about their task and angry enough with Aelish's incompetence to be credible when he spoke.

Aelish threw his hands in the air, "We're going round in circles Sael. We have discussed this again and again. I am shamed. I have allowed myself to act foolishly. Possibly incompetently." He paused and searched her face, "But given the circumstances, incompetence may actually be all that was left to do."

Sael knew she had lost and sat down, crossed legged, on the floor. There would be no ramifications for her challenge; except knowing the truth. The good of the Families sometimes could only come from the sacrifice of its families.

"I submit," she said, "The death of Ish as organised by you was for the good of the Families. The only one who could challenge you now is Ish, for sacrificing him without his consent."

"You are mistaken," said Aelish, "his death proves my competence. If he were to live then my competence would be destroyed and I should be replaced."

There was the sound of heavy footsteps beyond the tent and a hulking shadow paused at the door before stepping in.

"You bastard," said Ish, looking straight at Aelish.

The clerk burst out laughing.

# 5 AFSOON
## BY BEX CARDNELL

I'm certain she remembers the beatings. I wish she didn't. I wish I didn't.

Afsoon was never adept with weaponry. She can use a dagger, and she can fight with two swords, but every Hand can do that. They are secondary skills. Even a Ruqsandah is expected to be proficient with a weapon in each hand. They cycled Af through every combination of weapons possible. They thought for a while she might be good as an assassin, a Kahnjar, but after a few regrettable incidents in training that idea was scrapped. The more she couldn't make potions, the more she fumbled with weapons, the more she tripped over tree roots during training to be a Siyaah, the more they beat her.

I remember watching as the blows rained down on her and wincing at the dull thud of sticks hitting soft flesh. I remember us cradling her afterwards, gently washing away the blood, trying not to hurt her further with our soft cloths and softer words. I think one of the reasons Nizeh first started to learn surgery was to heal Af's broken bones, the poor fingers bent back until they snapped, to put dislocated shoulders back into place. Sometimes I believed what they told us, which is that the beatings were for her own good, how they would help her find her place among us as a true Hand. Sometimes, as I watched, I thought they just liked to hit her. We would bargain with the Kimiagar-in-training to get what balms and creams we could for her obscenely bruised skin.

Sapah and I would sit up talking late on those nights, trying to find a solution, trying to find a way to help her find her path as she slept tucked between Shamshir and Nizeh. We tried everything. There were nights the five of us barely slept as we tried to teach her the lessons we had learned. I can't help but smile, now it is over, at how many of my practice bows she snapped, or the time she nearly severed Shamshir's ear with a greatsword. It wasn't funny then, and we weren't smiling. We suspected that our time was running out; we were too old for another girl to replace her, and if she couldn't be trained in the ways of any of the types of Hands then we were all useless. Everyone knew what happened to useless Hands.

Sapah and I were almost frantic, desperate to keep our fear from the others, especially from Afsoon, but we all knew. They just didn't want to talk about it. Our teaching of Af became more desperate until the day that we had been dreading came.

We were in our room. It was just after dawn, and we had just finished bathing after another sleepless night of trying. We were exhausted. I had plans to catch maybe half an hour of sleep before the lessons of the day, but Matron Dash came into the room with a strange smile playing on her lips. We scrambled to our feet and stood in a line, heads bowed in respect. I found Nizeh's left hand with mine and held it.

"Today you are pitted against another group of Hands. It is a fight to the death, and you will undoubtedly lose. They have five girls who can fight, you see."

My shoulders slumped. This was it. This was what we had attempted to avoid, and here it was. Against five Hands, all of whom could fight, we stood very little chance, and we all knew it. Nizeh's grip tightened in mine, and I stroked the back of her hand with my thumb in a tiny gesture of reassurance that I didn't believe in for a moment.

"Grab your weaponry. Now!" Sapah looked at me incredulously. Not even time to plan? Time to talk? Time to say goodbye?

"But..." Shamshir spoke up, but at the withering glare of Mistress Dash her words died in her throat. So we did what we were told. Mechanically I picked up my swords, my bow and quiver. Everyone was doing the same, except for Af, who just stood there, head slightly lowered. She looked lost, and I loved her so much in that moment. I wanted to tell her that I would look after her, that I wouldn't let anything happen to her, I would protect her.

And I kept my mouth shut. I have never been good at pretty lies.

So one by one we trailed after Matron Dash. I know my feet dragged every step of the way. We were led to a large clearing, roped off around the outside, where a group stood, huddled and talking. I recognised them. Another Tyr,

a girl I liked. We would giggle together in class, sometimes.
Another Nizeh, Shamshir and Sapah stood there. Alongside
them Kahnjar. I knew and liked them all. My head was
spinning with the thought that these girls, who I was fond
of, whose fingers had braided my hair, would be the ones to
kill us. I had thought it would be a Hollow One. I had
thought it would be a teacher, or a Hollow One, or a
Grown Up! Not five girls, just like us.

I remember very little of the battle. I hadn't learnt at
that point to stay detatched, and I imagine that my actions
were a cross between a young girl with a little training and a
frightened animal. I remember the fighting being so close
that I had to draw my blades, I remember sweat dripping
into my eyes and then everything stopped. I was standing
and felt the cool steel of a blade against my throat digging
into the skin. I still don't know why she paused, why she
didn't just kill me, but in that eternal moment I saw them;
my sisters.

I saw Sapah and Shamshir fighting, sword and shield
working together so well. I saw Nizeh with two of the other
girls, teeth bared. Her spear moving faster than I had seen it
move before. And Af behind her, swords drawn, waiting
for one to get close enough to stab. None of them giving
up, all of them, my sisters, so fierce, so damn proud.

Af looked at me. Her eyes met mine and I knew that
the great drowning blue pools of her eyes would be the last
thing I saw. I heard one of the others scream my name, and
I closed my eyes to accept the inevitable.

It never came. I opened them as I heard words that
I didn't understand spill forth from Afsoon's mouth. I saw
the blue of her eyes reflected in the beam that struck the girl

behind me, in the halo of light that surrounded her. I saw something ripped from her body. I had time to gaze upon it and question what I saw.

"Is it her essence?" "Is it painful?" "Do I look like that inside?" "Is that the face that the Hollow ones see late at night, during those lessons?"

I saw the thing driven from her body, get crushed as if a mighty hand had come down upon it and the blade at my throat fell to the ground. Somehow the other Tyr was dead.

"Sister?" was the first word I heard Af say. In the gruff, breathy voice of the other Tyr.

I still wonder if, that day, when she became an Afsoon, was when her mind first started to crack.

# 6 FOR TYAN!
## BY ANDY SMITH

Omid, the Mayor of the town of Astara, had broken his fast on a mixture of dates and other fruits, along with a flatbread – a modest fayre for a senior Second of the family of Kade, but with the current predicament, Omid had thought it prudent to begin a rationing of the town's supplies, despite the town's affluence and stockpiles. Astara was located on the edge of the wastelands, in an area where several oases were within a few days travel, which had made it a prosperous trading town and way station for the nomadic groups that wandered the wasteland. As Omid emerged from the town's palace, his seat of power, the buildings and suburbs stretched out for a mile from the low rise his town was squatted upon. On the southern horizon, at the closest oasis to the town, a hulking mass of tents look like a blurred smear on the landscape; the Tuareg army that had sacked the city of Al-Faisal some three weeks before, that had been moving from oasis to oasis ever since.

Between them and his town, on the edge of where the meagre arable land gave way to the desert, a mass of earthworks had been raised, firstly by his people – upon learning the raiding army was heading their way – and refined and rebuilt by the Tyanite army that had arrived five days previously and taken over the defence. The army was small, only around a thousand men but it was led by none other than Bahram, the First of Tyan, The Great Tactician. The Tuareg had arrived two days later, and the armies had been staring each other down over the short desert expanse ever since.

Omid walked down the main street, towards the large encampment that Bahram had made on the edge of the city, making a note of which businesses were still open and which were still busy, working out which shopkeepers had slipped away in the night, and how the rationing was affecting the town's trade. As he emerged from the business district, he walked past the various buildings housing the Families within Astara, encouraged that many seemed to have not fled the prospect of battle. The daily business of the town wouldn't be too adversely affected, provided things went the way of the Kesh. As Omid approached the edge of the encampment, the sounds of hammers beating against anvils and metal scraping against stone echoed around the last few buildings of the Infirmary, where the Hollow Ones and the city's surgeons had erected their own tent city in anticipation of casualties. The Tyanites were great crafters as well as masters of war, and many of the men who would soon be standing on the front lines were now sharpening swords and mending armour. As had happened for the last five days, Bahram had sent one of his retinue to wait for him under the canvas tent closest to the town. Usually, Omid  only received orders on what men and resources were needed and where to place them, but today, Bahram had sent Farid, his second man and the leader of his cavalry, to meet him.

"It'll be today." Farid said almost as soon as Omid had stepped over the threshold of the tent. "The General is sure. He's asked to speak to you."

That surprised Omid; Bahram had, for the most part, kept the council of the Tyanites in his short spell at Astara. He had usually sent his lieutenants to deal with the senior men from the other Families, such as Omid and the senior NaBaal and Cyranus administrators. While some had taken offence at this, it had been explained that Bahram only wished to focus on the task in hand; the defeat of the Tuareg.

Farid beckoned to the opening in the rear of the tent and into the army's encampment proper. The cavalryman led the mayor down a long line of forges, many of which were gloomy without their fires burning, as their owners either worked the sharpening wheels and whetstones or were absent altogether – off to take their positions in the fighting forces, Omid supposed. For those who still waited for the services of the forge, the majority were dressed in the oranges and reds of Tyan, fabrics worn over gleaming chainmail vests and plate chestpieces, with veils tucked under helmets and chainmail coifs. A handful was dressed in the yellow cloth of Astara's Town Guard, seconded to the General for the battle. As Farid reached the final forge, he hesitated and moved across to a young boy, hammering at a red-hot sword on the anvil. The boy, barely out of his mid-teens, was already well-muscled and seemed to have little trouble with the strenuous task of weaponsmithing. Farid leaned over to inspect the boy's work, then motioned at something.

"Stop, Farouk…you see the discolouration?"

Omid stepped over, and looked at the hot blade along with the boy. Indeed, towards the base of the blade there was a thin line of slightly darker colour, almost as thin as a human hair, ran for about an inch across the blade.

"A crack?" the child, Farouk, asked, flipping the blade over to check the other side. Omid could see no sign of the discolouring on the opposite side.

"An impurity." Farid answered, "Not a major one, but it may weaken the blade if struck by an opponent in that spot. What should you do?"

"Umm…" Farouk's brow furrowed, "the impurity is close to where I intend to place the guard. Perhaps I could flare the blade into the guard?"

Farid nodded, clapping the boy on the shoulder. "That sounds good; the extra metal from the flare will reinforce the blade without the need to reforge it. Don't forget to compensate for the shift in weight, all right?"

"Yes, Master". Farouk turned away, reaching for his tongs to fetch more hot metal from between the coals, as Farid and Omid returned to walking towards the front.

"Your pupil?" Omid asked, hearing the clanging of Farouk's forge behind them.

"Yes, among others. He's my cousin by birth as well as being of my clan, so he's been sent to me to forge his first sword and begin his tutelage.

"So that will be his first sword?"

"Yes. Whether they make swords, gemstones or whatever else, a Tyanite's first  project is their rite of passage. It is the culmination of all their childhood education, their chance to show their potential and their ascension into manhood. If Farouk's sword meets my satisfaction, he'll join the ranks of the men of Tyan, to learn the linked arts of smithing, combat and surgeonry, as those of my family have studied through the ages.".

"Do you still have your first work?"

"I do indeed". Farid tapped the sword on his belt, sheathed in a black leather scabbard, with intricately etched patterns on the silver bands, throat and chape. "This scabbard was my first work, and it has been with me these last twenty years. It reminds me of home, and keeps me grounded through all I've done. I've improved the design over the years, as I've risen in the ranks, but it's fundamentally the same."

As they had been talking, Omid realised that the soldier had been guiding him to a large, open-sided tent, set on a slight rise in the camp. The position offered an almost uninterrupted view of the defences and their opponents beyond. In the centre of this tent, sat at a table, were two people clashing over a game of chess. The first was a woman, perhaps only a few years older than Farid, but the elaborate markings etched into the helmet resting at her side marked her as a senior member of the Army, a member of the Cyranus family and one of the General's disciples. Her tight-fighting armour suggested at a lithe beauty, but with her veil in place, it was impossible to be sure. Arrayed around the edges of the tent were some six other men arrayed in battle armour, almost exclusively dressed in the family colours of Tyan and Cyranus. To Omid's surprise, standing off to one side was a Kesh in the colours of Kade and an Orc wearing the ragged, sand-worn clothing preferred by the Earthmender Clan. Both wore light, mobile armour, but whereas the Kade's armour of interlocking leather panels was well oiled and looked almost new the Orc's armour was well-worn, with obvious patches in places and discoloured through years of use.

Sitting opposite the Cyranus was a man dressed in the rich oranges and reds of Tyan, with telltale glints of chainmail and overlapping plates of steel underneath. Even sitting, there was no disguising the man's bulk, his barrel chest speaking of great strength. Flowing out of the back of his veil was a mane of dark hair, tightly braided. There was grey mixed into the hair, the majority tied into a silver strip running through the centre of the braid. While very little of his face was visible, the lie of his veil across his features spoke of a wide face with chiselled features, his hazel brown, archer's eyes turning to fix Omid in his gaze as he stepped into the tent, the brown of a well-kept beard visible through the light material favoured by some of the more senior warriors. There were no markings on his clothing, save the burning flame of Tyan, but there was no mistaking the presence of the man. There was no question that before Omid sat Bahram, the Victorious, First of Tyan and War Leader of Akeah.

"Ah, Mayor Omid, thank you for coming. I had hoped for our first meeting to have been sooner than this, but as you can see, I've had much to do…" Bahram spoke with a deep, bass voice that made Omid feel like a child at his father's table.

"O-of course, First, you have caused no disrespect."

"Good…I trust Farid has told you the news."

"That the battle will be today? Yes, First."

"Please, I tire of that title. I am Tyan, a General, or I am Bahram. That is what the men call me, is it not, Farid? The Victorious?"

"Indeed, General."

"Well, F-General. It is great news to hear that the battle will soon come. All of Astara wishes you good fortune."

Bahram chuckled, moving a piece on the board in front of him. "Good Fortune, huh? I will accept your fortune, but we will not need it. Do you play chess, Omid."

Omid's brow furrowed, not only from the General's question, but his off-hand dismissal of his good wishes. "No, General, I do not."

"Shame…we Tyanites study chess and other games of strategy, to teach the basics of tactics, to keep our wits and intellect sharp, and to tell us about ourselves; our strengths and our weaknesses. This here is my new Right Hand, Taraneh. She's Cyranus, so she has little knowledge of the art of chess, but as part of her training, I've been teaching her the intricacies of the game. Come."

Omid leaned over the board to take a look. Without knowing the  game very well, it was impossible to say how the bout was going, but he could see a comparable number of pieces that Bahram and Taraneh had taken off the board, so it looked like the student was holding her own.

"You see, Omid…half of the game is manoeuvring…moving your forces into place, or getting your opponent to move their forces where you want them, until the time comes…"

Bahram moved one of his pieces diagonally across the board to take one of Taraneh's; shaped like the turret of a castle.

"Check."

Taraneh quickly moved another castle-shaped piece across from the opposite side of the board, blocking the diagonal path that her tutor had constructed. Then followed a flurry of moves from both sides, which Bahram distinctly came out on top of. Once again, the piece he moved first had a clear line to what looked like the objective, a tall piece etched with the symbol of Cyranus.

"Check. I'll be back."

Bahram stood, with surprising ease considering his bulk and the weight of his armour. He walked towards the front of the tent.

"She's still learning, but already she's showing as much promise as her predecessor."

"May I ask what happened to your predecessor, General?"

"Heh, He was selected to lead the expedition to the lands discovered to the East. I was needed here, with the invasion of the Tuareg. Besides, he's not as good at chess." Bahram chuckled.

"But what has chess to do with the forthcoming battle, General?"

"Because that is all battle and war is…a game of chess. You see the host arrayed against us?"

Omid nodded, turning his gaze to look at the Tuareg army beyond.

"Them, us…we are simply pieces in a bigger game, with the lands of Akesh as the prize. Sure, there are bigger pieces…more powerful armies, other influential people like my fellow Firsts within the Five…but it is often the smaller pieces, that lesser players forget, that do the most damage."

Bahram pointed out toward the Tuareg. "This army, if left unchecked, would have caused havoc with the desert tribes and the larger trading towns west of here."

"My General…I'm afraid I don't understand…"

"Their leader…I wonder if he plays chess? He is a gifted commander, but too ready to believe what he hears."

Bahram turned back to the tent, and the assembled men.

"Do you know how I, and not one of Cyranus, am in command of our nation's armies, Omid?"

"Why, because you are the greatest tactician in Akesh!"

Bahram chuckled again, "that is true, but it is more than that. It is one-part tactics, one part command, as Taraneh will no doubt assert," He glanced at his seated Second, who nodded her head. "And one part the use of information, either to help us, or to hinder our enemies." At this, Bahram nodded to the Kadian and the Orc, who both bowed their heads.

"These two men, Ghasem of Kade and Grishul of the Earthmender Tribe, have been instrumental in this day. Since the sacking of Al-Faisal, the Tuareg General has been capturing as many of the desert tribes and the Earthmenders as he can get his hands on, and…'extracting' information from them. Where are the oases? Which towns and cities should we target?"

Bahram turned to Omid. "For the last two weeks, those captives, even under torture, have been feeding to the Tuareg. Feeding them lies about Astara being the lynchpin of the desert merchants, rather than a relatively minor trading town…no offense, Mayor Omid".

"None taken, First." Omid said, hoping his voice and veil hid thoughts to the contrary.

"And finally, the Earthmenders told the Tuareg to approach the south, where the oasis would be large enough to water their whole army. With their scouts harried by my cavalry, there was no way for their commander to find out the lies, and fell into our trap. Now he is here, faced with a force they did not expect, strong, entrenched, and waiting for them. They sit on an oasis already running dry from a few days of use. So now he has a choice. Turn and run, and even if he outruns us, his army won't outrun their thirst. Or he can fight a superior foe, and hope to win. But that's not going to happen, is it, men?!"

The roar of "NO!" echoed from the men in the tent.

"Go to your units, and prepare them for battle. Today we stain the sand red with Tuareg blood, a tribute to our Lord Tyan, the Destroyer! FOR AKESH!"

# 7 THE FINAL LESSON
## BY PIPPA BELL

Nadira moved quickly through the bustling streets, expertly passing between people, carts and stalls. Market day was always busy and today was no exception. The dusty road was filled with bright colours and mouth watering smells; silks and threads hung down, bundles of plants dried in the sunlight, and grinning men stirred large pots of exquisite food, all hoping to trade and barter. Goats bleated impatiently from crude pens and birds scratched at the dirt, hoping to find some scraps. Nothing was still around her and as she looked back, the path she had made was even now being filled with more people. "As it should be," She thought, "I was there but they are not really aware of it."

Normally she loved the market, but today Nadira had more important things to attend to. She had been summoned by her master, Ekrim, to the great library of Nabaalasan and she knew better than to be late. She turned a corner and hurried up the grand stairs, ducking into the cool building. The noise from the streets was barely noticeable here and as the familiar sense of peace and belonging washed over her, Nadira almost forgot what was outside. The walls were lined with scrolls and ledgers; some held great stories, others official histories of groups within Akesh, while yet more contained lists of almost anything imaginable. She walked quietly through the halls and into a small enclave where a man was sitting, a collection of books laid out in front of him. He glanced up and nodded at her, gesturing towards a seat. She bowed her head and moved around the table, neatly placing her books down next to her.

"It is good to see you well, Nadira," Ekrim said, barely glancing up, "we have much work to do before you leave, this will be the last time we meet. While you study in these walls your mind is sharp, but when you are travelling, be wary of distraction. It is of great importance that you see everything, we must have accurate records."

Nadira nodded, "Yes Master, I understand what is required of me. I have made all the preparations that you asked." She opened a book to show a neat list of names and numbers, with a carefully drawn symbol on each row. "As you asked, a full list of alchemical herbs and plants, I have taken the liberty of listing them according to their base elements." She carefully turned the page to show more lists, "The following pages are the finished products, separated into balms, salves and potions, and then again into uses. I hope this is satisfactory?"

Ekrim looked at the pages, checking for mistakes and inconsistencies. This was merely a formality, a test of sorts, but it was important that it was accurate. "It is satisfactory," he said at last. "It is essential that you document everything you see on your travels. You will be the first to make these records and inaccuracies should not be tolerated. We must know what is available in these foreign lands, our alchemists will find great uses for new and curious ingredients, but only if you detail them adequately. It will be up to you to read their elements, you must be confident in your abilities. Do not be quick with your decisions, some of our documents show that it may take many days of study before an answer is provided." Ekrim knew that Nadira was a good student with a keen mind, but he was wary of her youth and the excitement likely to be found in this unprecedented journey. It was important for the Kesh that this expedition did not fail, and, as far as he was concerned, the childish fancies of a young Nabaali alchemist had even less importance than they would at home.

Nadira sensed the uncertainty in his tone and tried to hide the indignation in her eyes. She understood the importance of her role; she would not neglect her duties. But to be able to walk unmarked paths and pick unknown flowers? To be able to create rather than to just follow strict instructions laid down on ageing scrolls? Her heart was torn between her duty to Nabaal and to the other clerks, and her curiosity as an alchemist. "I am aware of the importance of certainty, Master. I am confident the coven will succeed, we have many great minds travelling with us, and I'm sure we will work together well. I will perform my duties to the best of my abilities."

"Their minds may be great, child, but they will not

concern themselves with the records. They are not like us, their minds are easily distracted and they care more for actions than words. You are the one who will hold the knowledge, and without you they will struggle."

Nadira expected this; it was common to have a poor opinion of those outside of Nabaali circles. She knew her role within the expedition, or even within the coven, would not be remembered. Her name would not be passed down as a great warrior or powerful mind. She was there just to see things, as others had done before her and as more would do after. The clerks of Nabaal are the bindings that kept the pages of the Kesh from falling apart, they arrive first and leave last, and while they have few of their own, they are aware of the words and actions of everyone around them. They stay in the background unless asked forward, and keep safe the information shared. This knowledge must be recorded, kept safe for those who come after us, for those who were not there. The clerks' duty is to ensure that every word, every detail, every decision is written down, for the good of the Kesh.

She gathered her books around her, bowed to her master one final time and walked smartly out the library, back into the hot, busy streets. She passed through the market slowly this time, pausing at a small stall to look at herbs. She found a flat-bread in her bag, wrapped carefully in cloth to protect it. She offered it to the woman behind the stall and held up a small bundle of white flowers. The woman took the bread and nodded. Nadira bowed her head in thanks and walked away with her prize, filling her senses with the spicy, earthy aromas that she knew she would now always associate with home.

# 8 HOLLOW ONE
## BY BEX CARDNELL

I NEVER WANTED THIS. I never thought I would come to this. I never thought that this would happen to me. Oh by the very Five themselves. I am so fucked. So very fucked. I never thought that something like this would happen.

I look at my hands, and I try not to panic. There isn't time to panic. I must think. I can't believe that I have done something like this.

The simplest of mistakes. By Tyan, I am stupid sometimes. By Cainen, by Kade. Shhhhhhhhhhhh. Think. Think calmly. Do not just take that hammer and bash in this stupid head. Do not. Pause.

Breathe. Assess. There is shame. Yes. Great shame. By the Essences, yes. What can I do to stop people finding out? Think. Fucking think. Wash your hands. Take the jug, careful, use a cloth to cover the handle, that can be burnt later, then pour the water.

Don't spill it!

There. Both hands clean now. Pour away the water. The pink colour will give you away. Can I hide this? Can I blame it on another? No. Think! Burn the cloth. Now sit. Look calm. Be calm.

But...No. Stop. Don't panic. Think. To run? They will catch you. And then what? Judgement. There is no way this is good. Then death. My body won't even be sanctified. There is no way now I can ascend. My soul will not join with The Essences. Calm. Think. Slowly.

Wait. Is that it? My soul isn't going to go to the Essences...

Softly. Quietly. Is that an idea? Don't pace like that. Sit. Back. Down. You're annoying me now. Have a drink. Some wine. Don't drink that fast. Calm. Calm. Soul.

Could I maybe?    But they are not like me. Shhhhh. Fucking think. I'd have to be better. Would it make me better? To give it up, though. Given up already when this happened.

Arrgh. A way out?

In the darkness of the tent the candle light flickered on the tent walls. A slight figure, shoulders hunched, a goblet in one hand paused in her pacing.

If you had strained to hear, you may have heard the question she whispered: "Hollow?"

## 9 A COMMON COLD
### BY STEWART HOTSTON

Hespeth clawed at the glass retort as it slipped from his hand and slowly tumbled toward the ground. Staring at the shattered vessel he looked up at the sky, stamped his feet and swore, "Desert cursed rain, why can't you just stop?"

Jahanda was watching from the edge of the mezan and chuckled, a harsh mocking tone that cut through the fruity smoke of the sheesha pipes. "That was worth two of those silver discs the barbarians hereabouts are so attached to Hespeth. They don't grow on trees you know."

"More's the pity," muttered Hespeth and poking at the glass with his sandal turned and walked to stand by the First of Cainen. "You should get me more. Some cloth too, to keep everything dry." Jahanda nodded, puffing deeply and seeing how far he could blow steam out of the Mezan and into the rain.

"I'll find you a broom as well, wouldn't pay to upset

the Voice would it." Jahanda wasn't asking Hespeth's opinion on the matter and, taking the hint, the alchemist returned to the shards of his retort and started gingerly picking them up between thumb and forefinger.

"I have an idea!" said Jahanda who had slithered to the family's lounge and laid himself out almost horizontally in one of the corners. Glancing around Hespeth could just about make out small stirrings of smoke dissipating in the warm air. "Well, do you want to hear it?"

"Not really," said Hespeth.

"Of course you do," said Jahanda, "These Lions seem to have a handle on the lands round here. I'll see if we can't trade them some more of our metals for what you need."

"That's your idea?" said Hespeth, wondering how such a dimwit ever became First of Cainen.

"Just listen," hissed Jahanda, "why don't you ask one of the clerks to cast some sort of drying spell over your equipment. That way you won't drop it every time it gets damp."

"It's always damp!" shouted Hespeth, standing up and turning to face the spot where he thought the First was reclining. "I can't move for sodding rain, for rivers appearing outside my tent's entrance, for clothes left to dry that are wetter than when they were washed in the river. There's water in the ground, on the ground and in the bloody sky. "I can't create distillates because I can't keep flames alight. I can't reduce herbs to powders because they're too wet. All the time it's wet."

"Calm down man," said Jahanda, "you're missing the main point aren't you."

Hespeth grit his teeth and waited for Jahanda to make his point. "If one of your NaBaalis starts enchanting your gear you'll never get anything brewed you great clot. Then you can blame the enchanter for the breakages! Simple."

Hespeth sighed and imagined he could see Jahanda's grin in the gloom, *by NaBaal's officious check lists he's an annoying man. I shall just ignore him.*

Jahanda quickly grew bored and found someone to play backgammon with, not that his inattention made Hespeth any happier. The alchemist stood at the entrance to the mezan for a long time dreaming of home and listening to the patter of rain on the leaves of the trees in the glade they'd set up camp in.

"I think we would see through such subterfuge," said a voice so arrogant and self satisfied it could only be AnBaal. Hespeth sighed and greeted his First.

"Indeed Hespeth. I would greet you too except it's wetter out there than a fish's arsehole and I prefer my water to stay on the ground not to fall on my head." The First of NaBaal huffed, adjusted the gigantic purple leather ruff around his neck and traipsed over to sit next to Jahanda.

"Hespeth," said AnBaal in a louder voice, partially obscured as he chewed on roasted almonds, "Sod off, I've got business to discuss with Jahanda. Take some of the Tyanites with you and go see if you can't find a reliable glassmaker."

Hespeth finished cleaning up the splinters of glass as the sound of the Voice drifted through the camp. *At least I'll be gone before his smell arrives*, thought Hespeth, trying to take what small consolation he could from being asked to leave camp during the downpour. *However, I'm not going to be all that popular when I tell the Tyanites that someone's going to have to accompany me to the Lion's village further down the valley.*

Amar, the first of Tyan in the New World, was sat under a large canvas awning with a handful of his men. Amar didn't care who he spent his time with, he respected neither rank nor competence. In Hespeth's experience the huge and grizzled general preferred people who would listen to his stories and trade their own back. He also liked pickles. Pickled cucumber, pickled lemons, pickled chilli and last but definitely not least, pickled eggs. Hespeth shook his head at the thought of the damage those eggs could do on their way out of the Voice – the carnage was almost indescribable. Amar always seemed pleased with himself after such an explosion occurred. *Which tells you almost everything you need to know about the man*, thought the alchemist.

"NaBaali," said Amar in greeting as he approached. Hespeth took it as a welcome and found the quartermaster, another Tyanite by the name of Sul. He was a smith and Hespeth felt they had some common ground.

"Hespeth," smiled the young warrior, wiping water away from his eyes, "My First is holding our daily gathering."

*Which explains why half of you are stood soaked to the skin,* thought Hespeth.

"What can I do for you?" asked his friend.

"Can you round up some guards, we've been told to go find a new glass blower." Hespeth shrugged as if it was a burden he had been lumbered with. He didn't want to be blamed for getting people wet and chilled to the bone. *It wouldn't be quite so bad if the rain were at least warm.*

"I know, I know" He rolled his eyes in response to Sul's look of disbelief, "Jahanda and AnBaal have asked me to do it."

At the mention of the two most conniving Firsts of the Five, Sul clamped down on whatever he had been going to say and, holding his hand up as a sign for Hespeth to stay exactly where he was, he slithered into the ranks of his Family.

Hespeth thought about going and finding shelter under a tree but the drips coming off them were larger than anything coming from the never ending bank of clouds above. He ground his teeth as he waited for Sul to return.

When his friend did return it was with two other Tyanites. Although the armies of the Families were not exclusively Tyan in composition Amar had gone out his way to select Tyanite Kesh to accompany him to the New World. Something had happened in the homeland which wasn't spoken of but the singling out of so many of his own kin had a definite whiff of paranoia. *Or incompetence.*

"This is Suhrab and Tousin." The two greeted him with their customary bear hugs. "We fought together against that undead witch and the walking trees."

"Do you expect trouble?" asked Hespeth hesitantly.

"Nah," said Tousin, "we're just bored."

"Getting wet's better than sitting here doing nothing all winter," said Suhrab as they shuffled back to the Mezan.

"Five turns of the middle timer," said Suli, the timekeeper and Notary to the Firsts, as they reached the

Mezan.

"What?" said Jahanda, "Rubbish, it's four and not a grain more."

Silence filled the marquee. "Five turns of the middle timer," said Suli again, his voice full of gravel and uncaring for the disagreement by the Cainanite.

"You'd do better not making bets than losing them Cainen," said AnBaal, "Now hand over your letter home, I wish to read it before Ka'am arrives." Jahanda handed over a small folded envelope and muttered under his breath.

"Need I remind you Cainen that we never open your letters," said AnBaal, a note of irritation entering his voice, "how could we function if the Clerks could not be trusted with all the secrets we have."

Hespeth had no idea what they were talking about but saw the delightful young body of Kasha, the mistress of their alchemical coven, reclining a few feet away. She was gently and rhythmically shaking a sealed flask. She saw him at about the same time and beckoned him over, "They were betting on how long it would take you to come ask for some of the metal discs."

"Of course they were," said Hespeth and ignored them as Jahanda decided he had found another wager on which he could double down with AnBaal.

"Don't worry," she said, "They've already given me half a dozen of the golden ones with a hole in the middle." She handed over a small pouch, "Be careful with it, you know how expensive glass is here."

"I know," said Hespeth, "They've got no natural fire and no sand. How they even discovered it is a mystery to me."

Before he could leave she pulled at his sleeve, her eyes sparkling as she said "If you see that fine young knight from the Lance by the name of Ser Owen will you ask him to come visit?"

He nodded and stood up straight, leaving the Firsts arguing over the terms of their next bet. He respected AnBaal's cunning but Jahanda was the First of Cainen for a reason and he wasn't sure who'd come out on top. *It's an interesting method for staying sharp*, he thought as they left camp and made their way down the valley to the village they had been trading with over the last few days.

"What the hell are you supposed to be?" asked the guard on the gate. Before Hespeth could answer the soldier started snorting in air and hawking up a glob of phlegm that landed at his feet in a bright green lump.

"This is Hespeth NaBaal, alchemist of Akesh. He is here to trade," said Tousin proudly.

The guard looked the Tyanite up and down, "Is he now? And I give a shit because?"

Sul put a calming arm on Tousin. Hespeth, seeing their chance slipping away, leapt into the discussion, "You care because I can clear your nose and throat so you can breathe freely."

"You can?" asked the guard at the same time as Suhrab.

"Of course he can," said Sul as if it was what Hespeth had been born to do.

The guard gave Hespeth a second, more calculated once over and lowered his pike, "How much does it cost?" he asked, not relinquishing his suspicion just yet.

The first time someone from the New World had asked Hespeth this question he had genuinely been lost but he knew what was required now and he had figured out a way of giving these people what they wanted without giving up his own principles.

"If I help you breathe more easily then you might consider letting people know that if they bring me lycopodium and arnica I can do the same for others. Otherwise I couldn't possibly charge a man who's keeping his people safe." Hespeth bowed at the waist as a sign of respect, making sure to give it as much flourish as his damp stiffened joints would allow.

The guard looked at Tousin, one soldier to another, "Is he taking the piss?"

"Not at all, this is our way," said Tousin firmly and nodding respectfully.

"Your way," said the guard flatly.

"Of course," said Suhrab, "no soldier who guards our people would ever be treated with anything less than respect. The job is arduous, tedious and demands a warrior to be alert come the harshest weather or the most mind numbing boredom. Not many can do these things."

"You're not wrong," said the guard with sudden conviction.

Hespeth meanwhile had been digging through his bags looking for the salve he had developed just for the type of head cold the guard was suffering from. "We don't get these back home, I'm sure it's your damned weather that brings it on." He pulled the stopper from the leather gourd and sniffed tenderly, the stench rising from its neck confirming it was the right one.

"By Melaphine's rotting lady cabbage that's rank," said the guard, taking a step away as Hespeth approached.

Hespeth sniffed irritably, "I invented this concoction in a single night. It works. I haven't had time to make it pretty for the big man with the pike." The guard was backing away as fast as he tried to close in. Sighing he reached back into his pouch and pulled out a small lump of sugar.

"Ok, this is sugar. You know what that is?" he snapped.

"No need to be arsy with me mate – you're the one trying to poison me," said the guard.

Hespeth made a show of pouring a few drops of the foul smelling salve onto the whitish lump and then held it on the palm of his hand toward the soldier. "Just close your eyes and once you've eaten it try breathing through your nose."

Suhrab, Tousin and Sul watched as the guard gingerly took the cube and peered at it. Just when they all thought he'd not go through with it he tossed it between his yellowed teeth and crunched. His eyes started to water and they saw him shiver violently.

"Do you think he'll throw up?" Sul asked Hespeth.

The alchemist pursed his lips, "I really hope not."

"I suppose so," said Sul, his tone suggesting that he might quite enjoy watching the spectacle.

The guard coughed once, wiped his eyes and took a huge gulp of air. He then breathed out through his nose. Hespeth couldn't stop himself from smiling at a job well done. The guard then wheezed asthmatically, gasped and bent over, hands on thighs. The four Akesh stood and waited.

Sul nodded at Suhrab and said, "C'mon we can go in I think."

"You're sure he's ok?" asked Tousin uncertainly.

Hespeth laughed, "He'll be fine. Had the same effect on me the first time." *I might have put a drop too many on the sugar, but I'm sure he'll be ok.*

As they made to move the guard held out an unsteady arm to block their passage. They stopped uncertainly.

"I can't let you go in," said the guard.

"What?!" said Suhrab indignantly.

"No. No. I will take you in." He stood straight and put a hand on each of Hespeth's shoulders, "You've cleared my snozz and that's three decades in the wishing. You won't go anywhere today without me as your escort." He beamed.

Sul exchanged a look with Hespeth and grabbed the man in a huge bear hug. "You are most welcome friend. We would be honoured to have you as our guide and companion today."

Tousin raised his eyebrows in disbelief but an elbow in the side from Suhrab kept him quiet.

"In that case," said the guard, "I should tell you that I am Corporal York and it's my pleasure to welcome you to the muddy cess pit that is Greenwood Village." He swept his arm out in an arc that took in the makeshift palisades behind him. Fitful fists of smoke could be seen rising over the wall.

Corporal York shouted at someone on the other side of the wall and the wooden gates began to swing outwards.

Hespeth's first impression was that the mud beneath his feet had been shaped into huts by termites fed on the mushrooms the Pathfinders were so fond of. The village appeared to have been slapped together and then allowed to melt in the rain. Straw roofs drooped forlornly as if yearning for the earth. In the centre of the village, built from wood and stone, sat a larger two storied building and it was towards this that York led them. The Corporal did not lead a straight path and they wound their way around the huts stopping each time someone came into view so that they could be introduced as the people who had allowed York to smell for the first time in five years.

"Truth be told I could do without the scent of pig swill and foetid horse dung, but after so long with nothing at all I'll take what I can get," he said as an aside between huts. As a result of his tour it felt to the four Akesh that the entire village was drawn out to see them. Children followed them around, some pointing and even pulling at the bright yellows and oranges worn by the Tyanites. The occasional glimpse of falchata kept them from being too bold but Tousin found himself smiling with pleasure at the obvious delight his appearance brought to these drab New Worlders.

As they approached the central building a voice called out, "Well it appears Solkar enjoys a joke as much as the rest of us."

Hespeth looked up to see a tall and pale soldier in chainmail with a red and blue tabard hanging sodden over the top. He'd seen the motif among the Warband of the nations but what this Knight of the Lance was doing so far from his army was a mystery.

"Lord Owen?" said Sul, "Am I right?"

"I don't remember you but I am indeed Sir Owen, please, don't call me Lord. It is not my right."

Hespeth was about to point out that no one deserved to be called Lord when he remembered the tales of Kimiia and AnBaal from the Round Table. These folk of Albion claimed some men were born above others and most definitely above women. Thinking of the water trickling down his neck he thought it perhaps better not to raise the matter. *Besides, this one doesn't even want to be called Lord. So where's the harm?*

"That you do not remember me is of no matter," said Hespeth, "it is enough that Kasha remembered you to me."

At this Owen's face paled further before flushing red. "The lady Kasha. I trust she and Kimiia are well?"

"They still have a healthy glow from their last meeting with you," said Hespeth mischievously. The knight of the Lance licked his lips and ran his forearm across his chin, "I'm glad. If it's not too forward of me, could I ask if they are nearby?"

"Not far, you may travel back with us if you wish, I am sure they would be glad to entertain you." Hespeth tried not to giggle at the man's discomfort.

"Um, no. No. I have duties here and once they are complete I must be away back to the warhost. Please, pass on my regards and say I am sorry I couldn't catch up with them."

Hespeth couldn't resist and said, "I'm sure they'll catch up with you in due course."

Owen swallowed.

"Anyway," said Sul, "Corporal York," and here he indicated the guardsman, "has brought us to you and we have come this far to find your smith."

Owen looked blank, "Smith? Here?"

"Yes," said Tousin, "although to be honest, what Hespeth actually needs is a glass blower."

Owen laughed hard, "A glass blower? Have you gentlemen actually taken in the grand architecture hereabouts?" York frowned but didn't say anything.

"I don't follow," said Tousin.

"You sirs are in the back of beyond. The nearest smith is two days walk and the nearest glass blower...a week east of here at Canterbury."

"We have one that visits during Winterstide Festival," said York.

"And how is that of use to the Kesh today?" sneered Owen, "Who exactly is on the gate Corporal?" The Corporal threw a murderous glance at the knight and withdrew, punching Suhrab respectfully on the shoulder as he left.

They trudged back in silence and the dimming dusk. Hespeth's mood only darkened when he discovered Jahanda had won his double down. He had wagered AnBaal that the alchemist would come back with less than he left with. AnBaal was not pleased that his man had been less than competent and the alchemist decided the better part of valour was absence and avoided his First for the rest of the evening.

They were relaxing in the Mezan when Haki, the Hollow One, came running into the lounge warning them that an outsider was approaching. Veils up they were greeted by a shy and nervous Corporal York with two creatures more like Shab than Kesh in appearance.

"I'm sorry to interrupt you," said the Corporal apologetically when he was eventually sat at the edge of the Mezan, Hooka pipe in mouth and baklava in hand, "But I heard you saying you needed people what could work glass."

As he always did with new guests, Zalish was taking an interest, "Well, that is true, one of our alchemists is...somewhat prone to, how shall we say, breaking his nik naks."

"So I wondered if you might be wanting to meet these what I brought with me."

The Elves, as they called themselves, had remained standing throughout and appeared to be waiting for something. What it was Hespeth couldn't fathom.

"Are you glass workers?" he asked them.

They nodded and said, in their strange lilting accents, "We aren't from here but you are lucky that we winter in this part of the world when the fancy takes us. We have heard of you from King Matalossi. He spoke highly of you and so we would offer our services in trade for something you might do for us."

An audible sigh spread throughout the room; these people knew what was expected. They might even be civilised. Jahanda appeared from nowhere and said, "A trade. Excellent. If you'll come with me we can discuss terms."

# 10 THE ISLAND JOB
## AKA KOOSHA'S 7
### BY RICHARD GEORGE

Koosha wouldn't trust Ugrasheer to watch his cook pot let alone the most vulnerable area of the whole dam compound! The last time he trusted "one of them" he acquired his limp. Koosha never made the same mistake twice. The Gulkorg was brave though. You had to give him that… and dim enough to not see past his nominal role in the plan. The diminutive Zahir was assigned the task of observing and studying the compound. For three nights running he haunted the perimeter. Observed every detail, every habit, every weakness.

There's always a way. Always.

By the end of Zahir's second report Koosha had the plan. A seven man job. If the marks followed their script and nobody fucked up then it could be done. There's always a way.

It was quite beautiful really. Art. Koosha *was* an

artist. His paints: his crew. His brush strokes: eventualities. His subject matter: human nature. His masterpiece: the acquisition of the single largest tree felled in the lands of Akesh for a generation.

And for the love of the five, that tree was huge! It must have stood two hundred feet tall before the destruction of Abadan and the reckoning of the Lord of Body many generations earlier. It was in all likelihood older than the oldest of the Shab who inhabited the coastal village above which the tree stood sentry, like a towering patriarch on its rocky, cliff top throne. Its fame was universal, its import to the Shab who revered it immeasurable… It would fetch a fucking fortune back on the mainland…Its felling would be heard for miles around, and the Shab are notoriously light sleepers!

After a month of tedious waiting, finally, the conditions were right. The brewing storm threatened to swallow Sheran, the island the Shab called home and their last vestige of autonomy from Kesh rule. The midnight broil sparked and mumbled as a babe might kick and squirm, eager for release from the womb. The outbursts tonight would be many and frequent.

As the rain fell, the team took to their places. At last, the storm birthed and the lighting began.

Quicker even than the lagging thunder, Zahir scrambled the perimeter fence. An intense flash serving to destroy the night vision of the sentry. Within moments the guard was downed. A surprised smile now echoed in the bloody gash across his throat. The gates were breached. The team was in. With an unexpected pat on the back from

Koosha, Ugrasheer lugged his siege bow into place and took aim across the village court. As the trio of greater elementalists made for the tree and Agraqope the pilot made for the harbour, Koosha detached himself and took up his place… in the cesspit to the side of the village Mezan.

The thunder rolled on, the lightening flashed, but as yet, the village slept. Things were going to plan.

From his foul vantage point buried waist deep in shit Koosha knew he had line of sight to the ship. The raising of the crude Gulkak banner from the jack staff signified that Agraqope was in position and all was ready. It was time to wake the village.

"Up! Up and Out! Gulka! Gulka! We are attacked! Up and Out!"

Another crash of thunder. Ugrasheer tightened his grip on the bow and cursed. He rearranged the bolts in his quiver and loosened the obsidian hammer slung across his back. Things must be really fucked if Koosha has been discovered, as must surely be the case. The alarm clearly came from the cesspit.

Within short moments the village was a hive of activity. Warriors emerged half naked and armed and all and sundry poured into the square to answer the call. Preeminent among them was a tall Shab, bollock naked from the neck down bearing nothing but a long spear and the circlet about his neck that marked him as the head of the village. Something else in his stance marked him as somehow different to the other Shab but all, in their preoccupation, seemed oblivious to its subtlety.

Curt orders rang out from the tall Shab; "Warriors! Form up facing the gate!" Protect the village! Beware Gulka!"

His long spear swept an arc encompassing the gate and the grassy mound where the Gulkorg was concealed. Ugrasheer tensed again as the wave of Shab advanced.

"Up! Up and Out! Gulka! Gulka! We are attacked! Up and Out!" Koosha bellowed at the top of his lungs.

As the Shab responded to the alarm Koosha's mark burst forth from the Mezan. From the reports of Zahir he knew the tall Shab leader was not possessed of greater magics and this lack of possession lead to *his* possession, as it were. Koosha smiled at the quirky irony of his internal monologue as he entered the leader's mind.

High on the cliff top, Farzi stood at the head of a three man wedge waiting for the signal. As the tall Shab motioned with his spear he knew it was their time. The wedge readied itself. As the lightning flashed they cast. It was not conventional to unleash magic missiles as a team but the focus device they had acquired from their anonymous patron permitted such methods. They knew they would only get one shot but the resulting blast should be sufficient.

They cast.

The base of the great trunk splintered and flamed but the stoic tree remained upright. Cries could be heard from below as some of the Shab noticed their sentinel apparently struck by lightning, but the wedge were oblivious to this, already zipping down the ropes linking the great tree to the tethered ships moored in the harbour below. As the tree flared, Koosha's smile widened. Things were still all going to plan.

As the three mages touched down on the deck they heaved to, aiding Agraqope in raising the main sail. The canvas billowed, the lines tethering the ship to the great tree pulled taught and, to the horror of the Shab assembled below, the great tree began to lean. The thunder crashed and the lighting flared and the base of the great trunk mimicked as it cracked and burned.

Down in the village the warriors were advancing on Ugrasheer's position. To his credit he'd not opened fire yet. This was also a good thing. Panic could be dealt with if necessary but it would be best avoided in the coming moments. The sand timer around Koosha's neck was just over half drained indicating that his grip over the spirit of the Shab Leader was running out. As the great tree began to slowly topple, Koosha played his riskiest card. Bellowing at the throng of Shab before him the tall leader gave his commands; "Hear me! Obey now! All elementalists form wedge! The tree is lost. Save the village! On my command levitate this doom away from our homes and into the sea! Time is short, obey me now!" As he spoke the bewildered Shab stumbled into action. Within short moments a wedge some fifty souls strong was aimed at the great tree. "On my command! Now!"

At the sight of the great tree slowly hovering towards

the cliff edge Ugrasheer stood up, dumb founded. As the first Shab warrior, semi clothed and screaming charged toward him he quickly regained himself and squeezed the trigger. The siege bow thrummed dully and the charging Shab fell silent along with two fellows unfortunate enough to be following in his wake. The enemy was so close now that there was only time to reload for one more shot, and this he did with practiced dexterity. The bolt hissed as it pierced the air dropping two more Shab as it scythed through the line. What *was* going on!?! None of this was in the plan! Flying fucking trees!! A panicked horror and sudden sickness in the pit of his stomach finally alerted him to two dreadful certainties; he had been set up and he was going to die. He turned and ran for the village gates only to find that they had been locked behind him. Turning slowly, his obsidian hammer in hand, he bellowed at his approaching end.

As the final grains of sand swirled through the glass, Koosha willed the Shab leader away from the others and into the cesspit, relying on the spectacle of a flying tree to draw all eyes and cover his absence. With deft skill Koosha dispatched the naked Shab before he had time to react. Executing him with a deep thrust to the heart from his curved dagger. As he retreated into the shadows and set off for the harbour his eyes drank in the scene; the giant wedge inching the great tree towards the cliff edge; the panicked villagers, crying, protecting their children and gawping at the spectacle; and the distant figure of the unfortunate Ugrasheer hacking and smashing in a hopeless last stand.

It was all going to plan!

Koosha boarded the ship just as the great tree splashed down. With a nod to Zahir who had just arrived from his back up position on the docks they were away. By the blood on his dagger it would seem that he had been wise to station a man on the shore. It wouldn't do to be recognised as Kesh, not if the subterfuge was to last. Prying eyes at this stage could damn us all. The storm winds blew, the tide ran out, the ship pulled hard on the ropes and the tree followed swiftly out to sea.

The servant of Nabaal gave a nod as he presented the parchment with the reverence demanded of the first of Cainan in all Akesh. He was a clever bastard that one, and with a flare for the dramatic, as evidenced in his extravagant attire, he would rise high in time. It paid to keep those sorts close. "Thank you, Anbaal. My eyes are tired, would you be so kind?" Anbaal unfurled the parchment and began to read;

"…despite the deaths of many of our people, and the loss of our sacred sentinel tree, one assailant was killed in the raid; a Gulkorg bearing the symbol of Isdick the Foetid on his back. It is the conclusion of this council that this attack be nothing less than a declaration of war, and we beseech the council of the five to permit a force of Shab on the home lands of Akesh to hunt down and destroy this foul Gulkak and all others of his kind." His rendering complete, Anbaal again offered the parchment for inspection.

From the reclined comfort of his cushions, the First of Cainan idly scanned the sheaf before responding, "My dear Anbaal" he purred "I thank you for this troubling news but this message is addressed to Kade. It is most unlike you to be so careless." He handed it back tutting, "You need not worry though, friends and secrets are like goatherds and water holes are they not? Thank you Anbaal." The bald Nabaali lowered his gaze but did not move to leave. "Is there something else my friend?"

"A fellow Cainanite, a man with a limp, is here to see you, First."

"… Is he now? Is he indeed. Well I think you'd better show him in then… and I wonder if you'd be so good as to remain."

# 11 THAT SINKING FEELING
## BY SI CAMPBELL-WILSON

As the boar came into view Taine drew back his bow taking a steady aim, slowing his breathing he could feel his heart pounding in his chest. This was nowhere near his first hunt - that had been many years ago but he felt a certain anxiety about this one. In three days he would be heading down the mountain to the land of the Kesh, with the other selected member of the tribe, to join in a great quest to far off lands; not that he was sure it would be a great quest, more of a chore having to spend so much time with the Kesh people. Taine pushed the doubts to the back of his mind, right now he had a job to do and that was to provide the boar for tomorrow's great feast. The shot hit but was not as clean as he would have liked and the boar ran off into the under growth, now Taine would have to go find the slowly dying beast.

The Terraka village was awash with activity,

people getting ready for the great quest, others just going about their daily business but there was something different about the mood in the village, something he couldn't really put his figure on. Maybe it was the anticipation of going with the Kesh or maybe it was the storm clouds brewing in the sky, after all this would be the first storm for months and it looked like it was going to be a bad one.

For a brief moment Taine thought he could smell the sea and taste the salty air in his mouth, but then he saw Maungaiti coming towards him, the Gulkorg yelled out "the Te'Khada wants all us to meet in the chamber of Caddoc, he wants to discuss the quest."

The chamber of Caddoc was a hot, hollowed out cave deep in the mountain where members of the tribe came to be at one with Caddoc, the spirit of the blazing fire of conflict. The tribal leaders met here often in times of war, or when the tribe had need of rituals - it was here that the Taniwha would perform them. As Taine entered the chamber the Te'Khada was sat in front of the great ritual circle with his first born son and the Te'Khada of the great quest Iharaira on his right, on his left was one of his best advisors Haimona.

Taine looked around and could also see Maungaiti seated next to Iharaira, this was no surprise as throughout the years it was always difficult to separate them and Maungaiti would not miss the chance for glory especially if it meant earning it with Iharaira. Taine also noticed Makutu, one of the great ritualists of the tribe. Toaiti, a

Gulka warrior, was sat opposite him and finally he saw the pale Haki, the one the Kesh called hollow, there was something about Haki that Taine did not like although he could not say what that was. Looking around he realised that this was not everyone who was going and he wondered why he has been summoned, "be seated Taine, we have much to discuss" the Te'Khada gestured to a low stone seat at the edge of the circle.

After several hours Taine emerged from the chamber into the fresh damp air of the storm that was coming down outside the entrance to caves. This is a bad omen, he thought as he made his way to where to other hunters where gathered around a large camp fire.

A young Gulka hunter called Aata came running over "What was said Taine? Which of the hunters is to join the quest? Who is leading us? Where are we going? When..."

"Not so many questions Aata, I am to select the hunters, and anything else you don't need to know just yet, for tomorrow is the great feast and I will make my selection before then. Now though, it's time for drinking and celebrating - for the next few days maybe the last we see of the tribal lands for a very long time."

That night Taine dreamt of great hunts and magnificent victories against the enemies of the Terraka when he was suddenly awoken by a deluge of water. He found himself clinging onto a wooden plank and all around him was the ocean, then he remembered the ships, the storm, in a panic he looked for someone, Makutu maybe or Aata, even one of the Kesh would be a welcome sight but there was no one.

Maybe this is what the Te'Khada meant by the Kesh are not to be trusted.

## 12 I SUFFERED
### BY ANDY SMITH

The storm was a cacophony of sights and sounds, even in the bowels of the ship. The rainwater sloshed down the hatchway like a stream; its path shifting with the roll of the ship in the swells. It made the ladders and deck slippery, despite the ballast sand they'd laid down for grip. The seas battered against the side of the ship, as if the hundred-or-so men were not at the oars, but inside a drum, being thrashed by a drunken fool of a drummer at some festival. Suhrab could feel the deck shivering under the ocean's assault.

The flagship of the expedition, the *Pride of Cyren*, was a huge, triple-decked dromon built for the purpose that, along with a handful of smaller single and double-decked dromons, had set off from the Homeland about forty days ago. Suhrab could remember seeing the *Pride* at the docks of Cyren Harbour; even though he was scared of setting out on the water, which he had barely seen since he was a blood-kin boy, he had marvelled at its size and its magnificence. Now, the atmosphere was claustrophobic and vulnerable, like a toy in a child's cleansing pool, with a full-blown tantrum underway.

"THIRD OF TYAN!"

Suhrab looked round at the shouting of his rank. There were four Thirds of Tyan on the expedition, Suhrab included, but Amar had seen them spread out one per ship, to ensure each contingent of Tyanites had a commander. Amar himself had spent most of the voyage in his cabin with his Shab. Many of the Tyanites had struggled with the voyage, the sea and the wood-built ships making fire anathema, and many - including Suhrab - had taken to drink and alchemical sedatives to make the journey bearable. But not tonight; he needed to be sharp. As he hurried over to the hatchway, he saw the Second of Cainan, Ardeshir, standing in the bilge below. The Cainanite was stripped to his waist and, despite the cold water spilling down the hatchway and pooling around his calves, Suhrab could see Ardeshir was panting with exertion and could see sweat steaming off him.

"Yes, Ardeshir?"

"The level of water in the bilges is rising! It's now at two feet and the men are struggling to keep up!"

"I'll inform the Firsts. Keep pumping, I'll send some fresh men to assist you!" Ardeshir nodded and disappeared under the deck without another word. Suhrab hurried back down the deck to where the majority of the expedition's men were huddled. Most of the Tyanites and Cainanites had been soaked in the first hours of the storm, getting the sails in and battening down the ship. Now, they waited for the eventual work at the oars, when the storm currents and the reefed sails were no longer sufficient to carry the ship onwards. They looked up as Suhrab approached, some warily, some with barely-disguised fear in their eyes. The Third glanced quickly over them, settling on a middle-aged man sat near the middle of the huddle.

"Heydar."

The Tyanite stood and moved to Suhrab, his muscles thick underneath his damp clothing, the exposed flesh of his forearms marked with the numerous small scars gained beating metal in the forges. Suhrab had known Heydar since he had entered the Tyanite Compounds, and had grown up with the grizzled, hulking smith.

"Heydar, take seven and relieve the Cainanites at the screw-pumps. I'm counting on you to keep the water level down, but inform me if the situation worsens." Heydar nodded, looked around and picked out six strong men and women, half Tyanite, half Cainanite. He paused when he saw one of the younger Tyanites, shivering against the bulkhead.

"Hey, TOUSIN! Come on youngling, some hard work will put the fire back into your bones!" Suhrab smiled as Heydar clipped the young Tousin around the ear as the men trotted over to the hatch below. Tousin was new meat, barely out of Temple, but Heydar had taken a liking to the lad. It was good to see such spirits given the circumstances.

Suhrab looked on in wonder as he clambered up on deck. His father, a Cyrenus, had been a fisherman, and Suhrab had been out in his boat many a time before he had left his blood-family. He had even sailed out in a squall or two, but nothing compared to this. Even though it was the late hours of Tyan, the sky was black as onyx as far as the eye could see, the sea a boiling torrent of grey, capped with white froth on the tops of the waves. On the port side of the ship, Suhrab could see the faint shadow of the *First PegAh,* one of the single-decked dromons that had stuck with them in the storm, a lighter blur against the sea, maybe a mile off. The rich light colours of the deck timbers were muted in the rain, and the blues and white of Cyrenus and Kade looked wan plastered to the bodies of the men and women working the deck. Most of them were huddled in the relative shelter under the helm deck. Suhrab made up the stairs leading up to the wheel.

As he clambered up the stairs, quite nimbly considering how the slippery steps were lurching under him, he could see Zalish and Amar; the two big men wrestling with the rudder wheel along with most of the Hands. All had their hoods up, sheltering their faces from the storm, but Zalish turned as Suhrab approached, straining to hold the ship's course.

"YES, THIRD!?

"Ascendant, water in the hold has reached two feet and rising! I've placed more men on the pumps, but we'll be fighting a losing battle if this keeps up!"

Amar had to shout to be heard over the noise of the storm. "Understood Suhrab! Keep everything under control down there and give us as much time as you can so we can ride this out!"

Suhrab turned to struggle back, when one of the lookouts on the right-hand side of the ship, suddenly started shouting and gesturing, his voice lost to the gale. Without a word, one of Zalish's Hands – Suhrab couldn't say which with their faces veiled – raced over to the lookout and, after a moment's pause, her higher voice, shrieking in her attempt to be heard, sliced through the storm.

"LAND! LAND OFF THE STARBOARD SIDE!"

Suhrab ran over, seeing the faint ribbon of land loom out of the rain bank a few miles away, a dark wet land that expanded outwards by the second. The Third was unable to keep a cry of joy at the sight, despite the circumstances. Finally, the first land they'd seen in five weeks and the hope of refuge from the storm rekindled the fires all but smothered in Suhrab, and he smiled at the Hand and the lookout. The lookout smiled back and, although he couldn't see the mouth of the Hand, the tell-tales crinkling around the eyes told him the young girls' emotions. Suhrab looked back, his youngling days coming back to him as he surveyed the coastline, seeing its shape…

The lookout saw his face fall. "What is it, Third?"

Suhrab, his face like stone, pointed into the water near the shore "do you see what I see?"

The lookout strained, but then he too saw it; the foam churning up in a line, running along the cost about half a mile from shore, as far as could be seen. The lookout turned, and this time he made himself heard.

"Breakers! *BREAKERS!*"

"WHERE?" Zalish's voice carried back.

"Along, the shoreline, Ascendant!" Suhrab and the Hand returned to the wheel "The reef stretches along the entire coast!"

"Essences, damn it!" It was the first time that Suhrab had heard the Ascendant swear, and it startled him for a moment. "The current is pulling us towards shore. I have not come this far to have it all wrecked now! We must break free of this current."

"Get below, Suhrab, and get the men to the oars." Even though Amar's voice was raised, it was steely and calm. Suhrab nodded and scrambled down the stairs, turning a slip into a leap for the deck. Seconds later he made it down the hatch to the oar deck and saw the Tyanites and Cainanites start at his return.

"Oars! Oars! *Move! ROW FOR YOUR LIVES!"*

There was a moment's lull, only a moment, and then the wood of the deck thundered as six score of men and women scrambled for the benches built into the sides of the ship, pulling oars the size of three men with practised ease from leather cradles strapped into the ceiling. The oar hatches were opened and greeted by the smash of a wave against the side of the ship, water gushing through the holes and drenching the Akeshi souls battling to shove the oars out into the stormy sea beyond. Twenty seconds passed...thirty, as one by one the oar teams yelled their readiness. Suhrab ran over to make up a team near the hatch left short by the men working the pumps, the notched oar slid into the lock with a satisfying thud, and Suhrab immediately strained as he felt the force of the sea against his oar. Yet as he yelled *"stroke!"* deck space filled with grunts of exertion as everyone began their own personal battle with the elements, with the fate of them all at stake. Suhrab yelled out the count, trying to keep time despite his muscles burning; he was holding his own, but most of his strength lay in his barrel chest and strong back, not in his arms. But it was working...

Time disappeared for Suhrab, he was lost in the count of the strokes and the heaving on the oar. When the beginning of the end came, the Third of Tyan couldn't tell whether he and the other men had been rowing for thirty seconds or thirty minutes. He felt his oar snag on something a moment before it was wrenched from his grasp, the poor Tyanite that he was sharing the oar with, a young woman called Salomeh...screamed in pain as her body was lifted off the bench, the oar whipping up. Suhrab heard the wet snap of bones as the force of the oar flung her against the bulkhead and the impact pulped her wrists. A fraction of a second later, the back of Suhrab's head exploded in pain and he fell to the deck. His jarred brain struggled to keep him awake, and the boat shuddering as Suhrab's world was filled by the plain in his head, the sound of tortured timber and Salomeh's incoherent squeals. A brief shadow flashed over his head and Salomeh's screams ended abruptly. Looking back, Suhrab's mind cleared just enough to see that all the oars on the right-hand side of the ship had been splintered or wrenched out of the oarsmen's hands. Most were missing altogether. Suhrab could see Tyanites and Cainanites nursing broken bones, looking dumbstruck. The unlucky ones were just sitting or lying there, unconscious or dead. Poor Salomeh was pinned upright, her pretty, serene face marred by the blood tricking from her mouth. Her feminine figure altered by the addition of an oar, lashed across from behind her with the force of a whip and embedded a good six inches into the side of her ribcage. The shouts were raised for the Hollow Ones, but Suhrab's mind was elsewhere, not on Salomeh, not on the others, but what he almost certainly knew was their doom.

"Essences help us" he muttered, "We're aground."

"SUHRAB!" Everything came back into focus within a split-second as Suhrab turned around and saw Amar climbing down from the deck, just as Heydar emerged from the bilges, dragging Tousin behind him. All three of them were soaked through, water dripping from their clothes. Suhrab could taste bitterness on his tongue, his surrounding slowing; "fight time", as his mentor had explained it to him, the body and the brain preparing for the fight. His strength returning, even surging, Suhrab hauled himself to his feet, his hand feeling the back of his head and coming away bloody. He was going to have a headache when this was all over, that was for sure.

"What is it, Heydar?" Amar looked questioningly at Suhrab, but turned to the grizzled veteran as soon as Suhrab had nodded – he was injured, but still capable.

"It's not good, First; whatever we hit, it's buckled the hull in the bilges in three places. Ardeshir's down there with the carpenters, but it doesn't look hopeful; the damage may not be able to be fixed in time..."

"I understand, Heydar. Keep the pumps working, give the carpenters as much time as you can to repair the damage. Take as many able-bodied people as you need, this is a priority".

Amar turned from the grizzled smith to his Third.

"Suhrab. Organise a work team to start moving goods up from the hold. Focus on the irreplaceable goods first; if we do need to evacuate the *Pride*, I want it done quickly, and with everything we need. You both understand?"

"Yes, First!"

"Then get to it. The Hollow Ones will see to the wounded once they've seen to those injured on deck."

An hour later, and Suhrab was wading in the waters in the base of the hold. Water had trickled down from the deck or through the timber walls between it and the bilges and gotten into the supplies. Although the water was only at calf height here, it was now waist high in the bilges, despite the frantic work of the men and women at the pumps., and the water had already done irreparable damage to many of the bolts of fabric, spices and alchemical samples that the expedition had included for bartering. Thankfully, not all of the goods in the hold were a total loss, and crates and barrels of weapons, tents, alchemical and crafting equipment had been hoisted onto the deck by Suhrab and his work gang of fifteen. They were with the Cainanite purser and his small detachment, who were making sure the essentials were all accounted for.

With a final cache of weapons winched up on deck, Suhrab clambered up from the hold into the rain of the night. The storm had eased slightly, but the deck was still being lashed with rain and high winds. The main difference to the vista was the absence of the *First PegAh,* still at sea maybe a few miles further up the coast. They had nearly suffered the same fate as the *Pride of Cyren;* caught in the same current, they had seen the plight of their sister ship and being lighter and swifter, had managed to pull themselves clear of the current. The *First* had tried to come to assist, but Zalish and Amar had waved them off as they struggled with the elements. Now, they were rowing up the coast, trying to find if there was a safe landing point nearby. There was no sign at all of any of the other ships that had made the voyage with the two behemoths, presumably scattered by the storm.

The other addition was the grey, rain-obscured land to starboard. The lashing rain still meant that much of the land couldn't be seen, but what could be seen was tall cliffs of off-white stone with some sand beaches at their bases. One of the lookouts had said she thought that she'd seen some lights up the coast in one of the storm's precious few lulls, but otherwise, there hadn't been any sign of life on this new, strange land.

"Firsts!" Suhrab's head snapped around at the lookout at the bow, her hand pointing forward. Out of the storm, the high bow to the *First* emerged into view, heading back towards them. As they neared, they made to turn away, their course countering the current. As Suhrab joined Amar, Zalish, Ardeshir and the Hand on the top-deck, the unmistakeable purple figure of AnBaal stood at the rail of the first, his hand cupped around his mouth. As he got close enough, his voice could be heard over the storm, faintly.

"Ascendant, can you hear me?"

Zalish yelled back, bellowing to make himself heard to his fellow First. "Yes, AnBaal! What have you found?"

"There's a break in the reef about half-a-glass further on. There's a beach, with what looks like some local vessels on shore!"

Zalish nodded, wiping the rain futilely from his brow.

"That's good news, AnBaal! Make your way there and pull in! We'll make our way there once we've effected repairs!"

Suhrab saw Anbaal nod, then turn and shout

something lost in the wind. A few seconds later, with the practiced ease of a fresher crew and an open sea to manoeuvre in, the *First* turned sharply and made her way north again. As the stern of the *First* started to disappear into the storm, Zalish turned to the group. "Okay, we need to get this ship - and everyone on it – half-a-glass up the coast without sinking. Ardeshir, how are the repairs going?"

The Second of Cainan winced at the question, which summed up the situation. "The carpenters have done what they can, but the collision with the reef has popped open one of the seams under the waterline. They've patched up the damage as best they can, but it's stemming the flow at best. In order to be repaired the ship will need to be beached."

Zalish cursed under his breath "Can we unload to ship using the small boats?"

"Unlikely" Suhrab said. "We only have the two boats, which will hold a dozen men each, maximum. Adding in the cargo, it will take hours, maybe even days, to unload the *Pride* completely. Plenty of time for this storm to flog us against the reefs. However, I have ordered the work crews to start loading the heavier cargo salvaged from the hold into the boats."

"Explain yourself, Third." Amar intoned quietly.

"There are better times for *kastiq*, Victorybringer" Ardeshir rumbled, shivering despite the heavy cloak he had donned, the long hours at the pumps must have chilled him to the bone.

"No, Ardeshir, it's okay. The heaviest cargo is also among the most valuable and needed for the expedition. Putting it ashore not only preserves them for the others, but will lighten the ship as well."

"A fraction, maybe" one of the Hands said, her strong voice identifying the speaker as Tyr, despite the fact that the Hands as a whole had adopted a look not dissimilar to half-drowned black rats.

"But potentially an important fraction. If we try to sail to this landing beach, a fraction more hull above the waterline could buy us minutes. Using the boats will also allow us to get some of the wounded off the ship, by giving them the task of guarding the cargo, we can get them off the ship and to the Hollow Ones on the *First PegAh* that much quicker." *and I get to stay here, and potentially save the entire expedition!* Suhrab pushed the thought to the back of his mind, lest it slip out, but there it stayed, the tantalising sense of glory on the horizon.

"Your *kastiq* is sound, Third" Zalish spoke quietly, but clearly, his decision putting paid to the matter. "Continue with the loading, and take command of the shore party."

Suhrab shook his head "With respect, Ascendant, I must decline. I do not intend to take the easy way out of this situation. I will stay with my men at the oars."

"Who are you to flout the will of the Ascendant?" One of the Hands stepped forward, hand reaching for the long sword sheathed on her back. Without thinking, running on the instinct of a lifetime on the training fields and battlefield, Suhrab's hand flashed out and locked around the Hand's wrist, keeping the weapon sheathed and squeezing the young girl's wrist enough to make her gasp.

Suhrab leaned forward, whispering in the girl's ear, even as he towered over her petite frame "Are you sure you want to walk this path, little one?" Pain flared in his groin, and the Third stumbled back gasping, his mind realising through the haze of pain that he'd managed to let himself be sucker-punched.

"That's enough, Sapah!" Zalish stepped forward, but stopped when he heard Suhrab chuckling.

"No, Ascendant, I deserved that one." There was a moment of silence on the top-deck, before Amar lost his battle with the mirthful laugh rising from his belly, and suddenly their laughter at Suhrab's discomfort lifted over the ship, drawing curious looks from the Kadians and Tyanites manhandling the cargo over the side.

"True, but that doesn't stop you being right. Who would you pick to lead the shore party, Third Suhrab?"

As Suhrab stretched upright again, the pain subsiding, he only needed a moment before saying "Tousin, Ascendant"

Now it was Ardeshir's turn to scoff "The youngling? I saw him at the pumps, a scrawny thing, with about as much sense as muscle."

"But with potential" Amar intoned meaningfully. "I see where Suhrab is going with this. We need all our able bodied men to even attempt to get this crate to dry land before we all sink into Cyrenus's bathwater. While Tousin is too small to be of any use at an oar, he has enough smarts to lead a party of men."

Zalish nodded thoughtfully, "Very well, Amar, see it done. Suhrab, get the men ready to take the oars. Once the cargo is off, we will see whether we are more competent than the elements."

The rain had finally eased as the two boats pushed off from the side, laden down to the gunwales with cargo and the wounded. Suhrab saw Tousin sat at the tiller of the largest of the boats, competently keeping the small boat in the lee of the stricken ship. Promise indeed; at this rate, he'd outlive all the other Tyanites on this ship...No, Suhrab chided himself, they were going to make it through this...

"Topmen! Prepare to drop the main sail, on my word! All spare hands to the oars or the pumps!"

The deck became a hive of activity, filled with the sounds of feet pounding on wood and the creak of ropes being pulled through pulleys. Suhrab rushed down onto the oar deck, already heaving with bodies, one third continuing down the hatch to the bilges while the rest slid onto the oar benches, unsheathing the remaining oars that were shared out equally. Normally only two men sat to an oar, but with some of the oars smashed to kindling and both watches at the oars, all the oars had three men at the oars, some had four, squashed together in this tight, tomb-like deck like apples at the bottom of a full barrel. Only a few men remained standing; Suhrab, chief among them, resumed his place as the chief of the oars, with a few younglings standing by the hatch, ready to relay messages or orders. "Right, lads and ladies! Ready your oars and prepare yourselves! Never mind the men above and below you, it's the strength of our arms that will see us good! On my order..." The deck fell silent, each man and woman preparing themselves. Suhrab could also feel the fire building in each Tyanite, the eerie silence broken only by the slow, synchronised breathing of nearly one hundred oarsmen ready to unleash their fiery energy to their task.

"Suhrab!" Amar thundering yell cut through the stillness from the deck above "you may begin!"

"All right, everyone!" Suhrab yelled, grabbing a beam to steady himself "3...2...1....*STROKE!*"As one, every person with their hands on an oar strained with a grunt of exertion, pulling at the oars, their force causing the timbers of the *Pride* to shiver and moan.

"STROKE...STROKE!!!...*COME     ON!*" Suhrab screamed, willing their wooden sea-witch to give up her embrace with the reef. Each stroke made the timber shiver and the boat squeal like a pig in the surgeon's training room. Over the grunts of exertion and his own yelling, Suhrab could hear the rustle and **WHUMP** of the sails dropping. For a moment, the scream of the timbers was unbearably loud, but then, the ship gave a little jump, like a girl being goosed by her first lover, and the feeling of inertia of palpable. The oar deck filled with cheers as the men and women, Ghulka and Ghulkorg of Akesh felt the fruits of their labours blossom, as their wounded ship took on the might of the ocean once more.

As the cheers died down, Suhrab handed over the counting of the strokes to one of the younglings. Walking over to the bilges, Suhrab stepped down the stairs, stooping to see down into the dark space. Over two dozen men hauled feverishly at the pumps, as water squirted in from a dozen different spouts through the damaged hull...an alarming amount of water. Suhrab saw Ardeshir and the other carpenters making hurried repairs; Ardeshir was slapping black pitch into one of the holes with a trowel, fighting his own personal war with the elements, trying to make the patch stick. The Second of Cainan glanced over at Suhrab's hail, but kept his mind on his work.

"How goes it?!" the Tyanite yelled.

"The repairs are holding, just about! We did some more damage coming off the reef, but we're staying on top of it. We're running temporary repairs as we go!"

"Will they hold until we make landfall?"

Ardeshir's hesitation said more than his reply "...it's going to be close."

Suhrab nodded, noting the look in Ardeshir's eyes as they locked on his. There was a look...Suhrab's mentor had told him once when he got too far into his cups on Tyanabad Red...a look of realisation, when your opponent or your comrade realises no matter how skilled he is...no matter how competent...that their match has come. Suhrab nodded, not saying another word, and climbed back to his post.

Ardeshir and his men fought the war with their hammer, timber, pitch and trowels for twenty long minutes before their luck, strength and skill were worn out, just long enough for the *Pride of Cyren* to come within sight of their objective; a gap in the reef leading to a small cove and a small, sandy peninsula. The hulking shape of the *First PegAh* was visible on the far side of the peninsula, hull down and already safe at anchor. On the beech, their visage smudged by the remains of the storm, were small boats, but boats nonetheless. Suhrab looked through a spare oar-hole, willing the ship on, when the crash of timber, raised shouts and the sound of rushing water echoed from below. Suhrab rushed over to the bilge hatch, looking down to see Heydar at the bottom, trying to haul a limp body up with him. Suhrab grabbed the stricken Akeshi, realising by the man's clothes that it was Ardeshir he was pulling up. As soon as Suhrab looked at the Cainanite's face, he knew it was useless...the handsome man's face had been pulverised. Suhrab looked back down into the bilges to see Heydar wading away, dragging struggling to the ladder, before disappearing.

"Heydar!" Suhrab shouted, but there was no sign of him, only a few soaked men crawling up the ladder, spluttering and shivering. The Third stood, and suddenly felt the gradient in the deck, starting to lean to starboard. Quickly, Suhrab grabbed one of the younglings "Tell the First that the repairs have failed, now!" Turning his attention to the oarsmen, the Third screamed "ROW, YOU BASTARDS!"

Not one man shirked. Every Cainan, Tyanite, Ghulka and Ghulkorg poured all their energy into the oars, their meeting with the Essence Lords at hand. Suhrab felt the deck shift as the *Pride* turned, making her run at refuge. But it was too late; as the ship turned, she listed even further sideways and suddenly water was bubbling from the bilge hatch, the weight of water making the ship heel over. Suhrab barely had a moment to realise what was happening when the sea reached the bottom of the oar-holes and started pouring in.

"GET OUT! GET OUT OF HERE!" Suhrab yelled, feeling the deck starting to shift under him, the *Pride* no longer afloat, but sinking...capsizing...Suhrab scrambled for a handhold as the water gushed in, soaking and covering the men closest to the hull, unable to move, unable to do nothing more than drown. Suhrab, among others, managed to make it to the hatch and hauled himself onto the main deck. Suhrab looked to the wheel, and saw Zalish and Amar fighting with the wheel. The Ascendant looked up, and saw the look in the Third's eyes.

"Suhrab?!"

"She's floundering, Ascendant! Ardeshir...First, there's nothing more we can do."

Zalish's face looked as pained as if he'd been stabbed as the realisation of their failure became apparent. It was a huge blow...the gamble had failed, and no not only was their ship forfeit, but their lives soon would be too. Zalish, nodded, and murmured something inaudible, but the screams of the Hands carried his message clear as a bell.

"Abandon Ship! Everyone swim for it!"

It took a moment for anyone to follow the order, but then Kadians, NaBaalis, Tyanite, Cainanites and Cyreni were rushing for the side, jumping into the water and swimming for shore, a tantalising mile or two away. Suhrab and Amar shared a nod as they both reached the rail together, hauling themselves over and dropping the few feet into the water. Suhrab's last view of the deck was of Zalish being pulled from the wheel by his five attendants.

The cold of the water as he plunged into it almost made Suhrab gasp, but instinct took over as he clamped the breath in his lungs to stop drowning. Pushing and kicking, he swam upwards and away, trying to avoid the multi-coloured flashes of other Akeshi hitting the water. He hadn't swam in over a decade, not since his blood-father had taught him, but Suhrab remembered enough to kick upwards, fighting the current.

Suhrab felt something grabbing at him, just as he was about to reach the surface. Looking down, he saw grey-skinned hands clutching at the clothes around his waist. It was one of the Ghulkorg, one that Suhrab didn't know, his fingers snatching at the fabric and his nails scratching and bruising Suhrab's midriff. There was nothing on the creature's face now but blind panic, no sign of the competency and dependability the people of the Akesh live by. Now there was only the bestial desire to survive in its eyes, and it was grabbing the only thing it could find, the Third of Tyan. Suhrab struggled to keep pace, and was losing, the current now in full flow and, with the virtual deadweight of the Ghulkorg clutching at him, the surface started getting further and further away. Pushing and kicking, or even attempting some cajoling into helping to swim did nothing more than make the thing clutch at him harder, ruining any chance for either of them surviving. Soon, Suhrab began to feel the burning in his lungs, the sand was fast running out of the hourglass.

There was no other thing for it. Suhrab's sword and shield, and indeed most of the weapons of the Akesh, had been sent with the shore party. But as Suhrab felt behind him, his fingers caught on the familiar weight of the dagger strapped to the small of his back. With a brief tug, the cold steel came free, and with a snarl, Suhrab plunged the dagger between the Ghulkorg's ribs. The Ghulkorg screamed. Underwater, the sound was muffled, but the blast of blood-tinged air bubbles that hit Suhrab smack in the face almost, almost made him gasp for air. The Third of Tyan, lungs burning, stabbed again, pushing the thrashing, dying beast away, as blood loss and drowning fought their battle to

121

claim the prize, the Ghulkorg torn between clutching at its throat or its wounds as it sank.

Giving the sinking Ghulkorg no more attention, Suhrab kicked for the surface, frantically trying to reach the surface before giving in to the need to breathe. Ten seconds passed...twenty...the surface in sight, tantalisingly close as Suhrab's lungs and muscles burned with the need for air, but still far away. Too far away. Suhrab's breath gave out and the cloud of bubbles disguised his despairing last few strokes, but the surface was still metres away as his vision blurred and darkened. Suhrab's last despairing thought echoed around his mind as the darkness and the embrace of the essence lords started to embrace him.

*I've failed.*

### *Rise...Rise, Suhrab...*

The first thing Suhrab noticed was the heat. The sea, the ship, the entire voyage had been cold, but now, it was like a clear day in Tyanabad, his clothes dry and airy as he opened his eyes. The place was bright, the colour of ivory. The floor felt of...*something*, it was solid, smooth like glass, but not slippery, as he levered himself to his feet.

### *Suhrab...*

The Third of Tyan turned, and saw the man stood behind him for the first time. He was big, the same bear-like size and physique of Amar, dressed in the opulent oranges and reds of the Tyan Family, the glints around the seams and buttonhole indicating the bronze scale mail underneath reserved for a veteran warrior. His face was a mass of ginger hair, bright as flame, with long braided hair and a matching beard. Only the man's chin was clean-shaven, showing a chiselled jaw under the fur. This man's voice was a low grumble, the sound you would expect a rock-slide to make.

*Do you know who I am, Suhrab?*

"I can guess."

The man chuckled, a deep bass rumble that seemed to vibrate in Suhrab's ribcage.

*Not what you were expecting, huh? Perhaps this might be more fitting...*

Suhrab had barely enough time to shield his eyes before the figure before him grew and...Ignited. Well...not so much ignited as transmuted into flame, the man's skin, hair and clothes becoming the different shades of the fire; his hair became the orange of wood-flame, his skin and clothes the whites and reds of the forge-furnaces, but his eyes, his eyes were the blue-white of the Heart Fire, the purest fire that Tyan had given to the Custodians of the Temples, which could craft the finest blades known to Akesh. The heat was like standing in front of an oven, before the flaming figure dimmed, so that he was still alight, but Suhrab could look at him again.

*How about now?*

"Yes, Lord Tyan...so, I presume that I'm dead, then?"

*More or less.*

Suhrab looked at the Essence Lord quizzically "What, do you mean, Lord Tyan?"

*I mean, that I have already taken many souls into my care this day, as a result of this ill-fated expedition. Those that I have taken into my care have spoken highly of you, Suhrab. Heydar in particular spoke highly of you, and he has earned his place of safekeeping many times over. Which is why I brought you here a little early...I have a proposition for you.*

Suhrab's mind was whirling...Lord Tyan, one of the five essence lords which Akesh had modelled themselves on, had a proposition for *him?!* "O-of course, Lord, what would you have me do?"

*Have you heard the saying in the old tongue: t'alimtu fat'alamtu fataghayrtu?*

Suhrab nodded "Yes, Lord, 'I suffered, therefore I learned, therefore I changed', it was one of my tutors' favourite sayings."

*And it is very apt now. For the Akesh, for the expedition, and for you...you are dying, the expedition is on a knife-edge, and the Akesh are stuck in a stalemate with the Tuareg. You all need to learn, and to change, in order for the deadlock to be broken and for Akesh to survive. While most of my power and abilities are focused elsewhere, in your case, I can tip the balance, and maybe, maybe give the expedition a fighting chance. Do you understand, Suhrab?*

The Third nodded "I think I know what you are planning. I will not insult you with *kastiq*, but is that the only way?"

Tyan nodded. *It is. Well, there is always death...I have offered this choice before, and some have chosen death over it.*

"I understand, Lord Tyan. But it is for the good of Akesh. Thank you."

*Oh, don't thank me just yet. Heydar also mentioned that you were an arrogant, ambitious young upstart who was as much impudent and arrogant as competent. Consider this a lesson. Are you ready to learn?*

Suhrab barely had the time to nod before the Essence Lord raised his arms and, a moment later, all was fire. The Third of Tyan screamed as pain flared within him, lancing through his bones. Suhrab couldn't tell if it was real or his imagination, but even though it felt like the pain filled its existence, he could still smell charring flesh and burning cloth, hear the crackling of the flames, see the flickering flames of the pillar that engulfed him. The pain rose, every second it felt like it wouldn't worsen, it did. But Suhrab was lucid, even though his mind was screaming with nerve impulses, fraying at the edges as the flames scouring his inside. Then he felt something give way, something...*torn* away and the flames evaporated. His leg unable to hold his weight any longer, Suhrab collapsed to the floor, feeling nothing but emptiness as he blacked out. He barely felt the fires engulf him again, filling him...

Suhrab woke with a hacking cough, water spewing from his lungs. The flames were gone, there was only the sound of the waves and the cold deep in his bones. He felt hands pulling him up, the gritty feeling of sand against his feet. Finally, his eyes started to focus on the faces of Tousin and Amjad Khali, the Voice of the Hollow Ones, who he'd met at the start of the expedition – he'd travelled on the *First*.

"Breathe, Suhrab!" The Tyanite gulped in air, coughing up a little more water as he cleared his lungs. Amjad managed a small smile.

"Good, you'll live. Tousin, help him up, see if you

125

can check some of these men, yell if they are not beyond saving!" Amjad moved quickly despite his massive frame, moving along the sandy beach to check another body dragged up by the surf. Suhrab was grateful for the shoulder of the youngling to hold to as he hauled himself of the sand, his legs as unsteady as a newborn foal's.

"How long was I out?"

"I don't know" Tousin said quietly, "the *Pride* went down about ten minutes ago. There are still survivors swimming ashore." Tousin pointed, and Suhrab saw a huddle of figures emerging from the surf, grey figures surrounding blue told the two Tyanites that it must be Zalish and his Hand.

"Come on". Tousin intoned quietly as he and Suhrab hobbled down towards the group. It was quickly evident that something was wrong, Zalish was kneeling, his Hands clustered around him. One, Two, Three, Four...where was the fifth Hand? There...between them all, with the Ascendant kneeling over her, was the fifth hand, lying unmoving. Tousin took one look and was howling for Amjad, now a good way up the beach, turned and started moving towards them.

*He's gonna be too late...*something nagged at Suhrab's mind, "Tousin, get me to her. Now!" The youngling started at Suhrab's raised voice, moving the slowly-steadying Tyanite towards the gaggle, trying to push through the Hands. They initially tried to stop the two Tyanites, almost without looking, but a barked command from Zalish made them part. The Hand lying on the sand, her slight, small frame identifying her as Afsoon, was a sodden mess, and only a moment's glance told Suhrab she wasn't breathing.

"She couldn't keep up" Zalish gasped, "She fought, tooth and nail, but she..."

Suhrab nodded, dropping to the sand and dragging himself next to the limp body of Afsoon. Sapah was fretting next to her; Suhrab knew she was a trained surgeon, but there was no sign of either hers or Afsoon's surgery kits.

"It's all right, Ascendant, I'll see what you can do..."

"What can you do, Tyanite?" Tyr snapped, before Tousin shushed her, his eyes riveted to his Third, placing his hands onto the skin above Afsoon's lungs.

The words flowed. Suhrab had heard them before, muttered from the mouths of Mendicants and Hollow Ones. He felt the words resonate in him, and a feeling of energy, deep in the pit of his stomach, twisting and growing at his will. He didn't recognise his own voice, guttural but clear, chanting...

"May the power of the fountain of life flow through me and bestow lesser healing. May the power of life flow through me and bestow lesser healing. May the power of the fountain of life flow through me..."

Suhrab kept chanting, feeling the power in the pit of his stomach surge through his veins and nerves, tingling his palms and his fingers and it flowed into Afsoon, a brief pulse of low light heralding each surge of hollow magic. Second later, the Hand shivered, and exploded in a fit of coughing, a stream of water issuing from her lips. Suhrab fell backwards, exhaustion finally catching up to him, as the Hands stepped around them to check on their sister. He saw Tousin looking at him, mouth agape, completely unmanned.

"Close your mouth, Tousin, you'll catch flies"

Suhrab chuckled tiredly, the traces of water in his lungs giving the chuckles a familiar bass ring. He should have been amazed, shocked...but the only thing that surprised him was how calm he was about what had happened. He knew that his time as a Third was over, and he did not know whether his power was such that he would have to become Hollow, but for now...whether through his meeting with Tyan or just simple exhaustion, he was at peace.

"W-what happened to you?" Tousin managed to stammer. The youngling's look of amazement made Suhrab chuckle as he lay on the sand, blessed sleep finally coming to claim him, managing just a few words before slipping into dreams of the Man Afire;

' t'alimtu, fat'alamtu, fataghayrtu".

# 13 HUBRIS
## BY STEWART HOTSTON

"C'mon Strid, tell us the story again," asked Ser Lucien of the Lance. The men and women around the camp nodded, smirking. Eyes shone with anticipation and bodies leant forward.

Strid sighed, "Really? That's the one you want? I might have been there but I only know what I was told. We didn't see her." He tugged at his beard as if he was considering refusing. There was no chance he would; he knew it, they knew it, but it wasn't done to simply launch into the retelling. The phoenix on his shield glinted dully in the fading light of the camp fire, sleeping for now.

Strid stretched his legs out in front of him, arms pushed back to support the weight of his body. "There was once a nation who had no gods. A nation of conniving, scheming, cunning foreigners who landed here and proceeded to change the world as we knew it. As with all who change the world, they were changed themselves in the changing. The Akesh." Around him the audience bent close to hear every word.


"You!" said Oak, looking furiously at the sniggering woman. "If I don't then the Goddess will rip your heart out if you start laughing half way through our ritual."

The woman covered her face with a hand to hide her lack of self control. The attempt was pointless, a veil already hid all but her eyes and it was the sound of her derision that had riled Oak. He sighed, closed his eyes and calmed himself. *I cannot lose my own focus. I am here for the Goddess. I am here to speed the recovery of our lands now the Capricious Queen is gone.* He cursed that the ritual needed so many people willing to contribute to it. At first he had even doubted the Kesh woman could contribute. *After all, she has no faith,* he thought.

Yet the Teutonians had vouched for her, as had that scheming madman in the purple collar. He thought about asking her what was so damned funny but refrained as he knew the bloody Kesh would explain it all in a three point sermon which he'd then be expected to either refute or accept her behaviour as reasonable. *They respect nothing except competence.* He grudgingly respected such a stance - it was a logical position to take for a people so far removed from the path the Goddess had put him on. That didn't stop it from being more annoying than a sober Fir Cruthen.

Oak ignored her and went over the ritual from the beginning. The other participants followed his lead and carefully rehearsed their pieces and movements. *We're almost there*, he thought happily. The honour guard for this event was composed of his former people, the Ael, as well as half a dozen lightly armoured Akesh in red and orange, their eyes peering through between veils and turbans. Stood at the edge of the glade were Strid and Brin, their studiedly weary expressions only half on what he was doing.

*Why did the Eored give the Kesh their city?* He wondered, *what were they thinking?* All he knew was that the negotiations had involved a fox, a tax discussion that left all but one of the clerks in the Kesh with a headache and a promise of deep sea fishing. *Where do I even begin with that set of nonsense?* Oak shook his mind again and, turning to face his community of priests, mages and other participants he said "It is the height of the day. It is time."

The twenty four of them filed into the circle of standing stones which looked like it had required ogres to drag them into place. At cardinal points around the perimeter were dolmens; immutable witnesses through which the Spirit of the Circle might communicate.

Oak raised his hands and asked for the circle to be closed. The Hunter so often needed blood; needed for his nature, his name, to be remembered in actions that were far from symbolic. In contrast, the Goddess was prepared to be honoured with actions that helped her people remember who they were. Oak was at peace with her apparent domestication. The Hunter was literal, his unpredictableness all too predictable. In contrast, the Goddess was nebulous, her purview so broad as to necessitate abstraction and ambiguity. Of the two of them she was the more alien, the more unreachable and in the end, the Goddess was far more discomforting for those who thought on what she was than the Hunter. *The mind that domesticates her suffers from a failure of heart.* Yet Oak knew, because the Goddess herself had told him, that a small mind can still hold a true faith. If the faith of the foolish was obvious in its errors they were to be honoured for their transparency. It was the clever whose failures were the more dangerous because they were so often masked by reason and power.

Oak walked alone with his Goddess now; he no longer called himself Ael and the faith he had nurtured then had been broken, transformed like slowly cooling lava into precious stones. If he no longer burned hot like his former family he carried a hard, clear and multi-faceted gem of belief that was his and his alone.

The ritual he led today was ancient and holy. Oak had completed it once a year for the last four years, although that short span seemed like an eternity. A small number of the contributors with him in the circle had been there each time, but the courts he travelled with moved almost constantly across the continent, and he had lost track of those he had conjured with over the years. The circles of the world were places of power; religion was second, third if the Fae of House Majister were to be believed. *Except they too have their agendas* he thought. Whether the tales told about them were true or not he didn't care. What Oak knew was that the rhythms, the ebb and flow of the circles, were not a matter of pulling at levers or completing equations. It was a path, a dance whose moves were mundane, everyday and repetitive. They were the flower blossoming, withering and falling to the ground dead only to rise again. The path of the Goddess was about the flower whose life was wasted, about the river whose course faded over millennia. The path of the Goddess was everything, and in the circle Oak found his all.

If there was one aspect of the Goddess he had truly loved it was the Capricious Queen, a symbol of the violence and randomness of nature. An icon broken so that the struggle for survival lost all its meaning. *The Queen is dead,* thought Oak and he moved to and fro in the circle, sliding between the others in a dance of life renewed and corruption purified.

As they neared the focal point of the ritual he could feel the hairs on his arms raised in sympathy with the power being gathered around him. He would find a lover tonight and they would both be exhausted by morning. The Dolmen on the eastern point of the circle rumbled, a deep noise he felt more than heard. It was far from what he was expecting but he was a master at sensing the direction the world wanted to go. He reached out towards it only to be knocked from his feet and pinned to the ground by an eruption of will and personality so immense he could not begin to make sense of what held him in its grasp.

The others ritualists had broken, most prostrate, a few managing to find a knee on which to push themselves away from the ground. They had the appearance of folk far away, hidden behind a gauze sheet; near but beyond his reach. Oak looked around and saw he was not alone in this separation, the Kesh stood upright at the edge of the circle, a look of fear and curiosity in her eyes, her body still like a night after snowfall. Outside the circle Strid and the others were pressed up close, calling to see if there was anything to be done; he was sure they could not see him.

Oak's mouth was shut by an invisible finger that pushed up into the soft flesh under his chin. He wasn't going to open the circle any time soon.

Looking the other way, the pressure under his mouth moving with him but not hard enough to harm, he watched the Dolmen. The entrance blurred, its depths like a lover's eyes.

A voice echoed around the circle, "Oak, my little one, how timely it is." He grinned in spite of the fear that seized him. *My Love.*

"Beloved," said the Goddess, "I am not yours to call 'my'." The pressure eased and he levered himself off the ground. She had dressed herself as a short woman, breasts hanging low and lines etching her face with age and wisdom. Her hair was long and pinned up on the top of her head, streaks of grey and blond shot through ebony. As he watched her naked form was covered by a black silk gown embroidered in spirals and labyrinths of green and silver filigree. He knew then he was in a vision; the Goddess never appeared in such a form - she was not like the gods of the other nations who appeared wrapped in flesh in order to whine and stamp their feet. The Istar was her representative, her voice in this world. To see the Istar was to see the Goddess.

"I do not thank you for your actions," she said. "Do not think I am glad about what has been done."

Oak had hated himself for the death of the Goddess' Istar, no one doubted he was responsible. "There was nothing else to consider. In the end."

"Be that as it may," and in her voice there was the sound of the hive swarming and the boar charging. He waited for her. "I can taste the confusion on you like rancid butter Oak."

He shook his head, irritated, "I'm not confused."

Her form moved, a languid and luxurious walk to stand in front of him. Where her feet touched the ground bluebells and posies sprang to life and withered with each step. "You are always intentional." She went to put her hand on his shoulder but held off. "I prefer it when you are free."

"You told me once that freedom was the capacity to accept what is and act anyway. The path has taught me that freedom is about understanding the rules instead of acting without any."

She sighed with a sound of birds taking flight, "Acting rashly is to test the rules knowing full well they are there."

Oak started to answer her but the words died in his mouth. The Goddess was gazing intently over his shoulder, he was an obstacle to be looked past. Turning his head he saw the Kesh, weight on one hip and arms folded across her chest.

"I have not seen you here before," said the Goddess. She moved away from Oak and walked towards the Kesh.

"Nazari. I have not been here before," said the Kesh simply, her accent thick on the words that came through her veil. "Wherever here might be."

"Are you someone's property that you must hide your face?" asked the Goddess.

"What kinship have you shown me that I should give you my face? What hostility have you undertaken that I should show you my face?" said the Kesh.

"I am," said the Goddess and, turning from the veiled woman, she proceeded to move throughout the circle, touching and blessing each of the other ritualists. Oak watched this, waiting for his turn, but she excluded him from her ministry. When it was clear she had finished he said, "Why have you come here?"

"Ah. That confusion again. It's not all about you Oak."

"Have you come to help us?" he persisted. *Having a god here is not helping us do what must be done.* He hoped that by pestering her they could move on and finish the ritual. If she would help all the better.

She ignored him, returning to the Kesh woman. Oak was impressed, the foreigner did not so much as take a step backwards although the fear radiated from her as clear as day. If the Kesh was sharing this vision he wanted to understand why. "I came because I tasted something new."

"You are not from here," said the Goddess to the Kesh, the emptiness of the freshly killed stag echoed in her voice.

The woman shrugged, "As you say."

"She is from the western continent," said Oak.

"Hush, Oak," said the Goddess, "All you know is what they have told you. Did they tell you which of the western continents they came from?"

He knew better than to reply. The Kesh woman looked at Oak and back to the Goddess as if deciding which she might buy; he wanted to warn her but she was beyond his aid now.

The Goddess paced slowly around the woman, sniffing and, at one point, sticking her tongue out as if tasting the air. "You have no faith Tenesther," she pronounced at length. "It tastes like copper."

The Tenesther turned to face the Goddess, who had spoken from behind her, "I believe in many things creature, but not in the right of others to invade my mind."

The Goddess took a step back. In the distance a fox howled. "The birds whisper your name Tenesther, the wind sighs it. It is not my way to impress myself upon the path."

Tenesther inclined her head by way of apology but said nothing more.

"You truly consider me a creature, a thing made. How is this possible? Have my people not told you of me?" She cast a sharp glance in Oak's direction. "I am. The path is the way of all flesh. Even for you, although you know it not."

"All ideas can be made so broad as to capture everyone," said Tenesther. "The trick is to define your terms tightly enough to capture exactly that which you seek but no more." The Goddess waited as it was clear Tenesther sought her acquiescence to continue. "Are you some creature claiming dominion over the forests of this continent, over the land or the sea? Do you claim the whole plane as yours? What about beyond?"

"Yes," said the Goddess.

The Kesh nodded as if that was the answer she was expecting. "The other Gods? How do their claims rank against yours? Are you senior, pari passu or junior?"

"We will be what we will be," said the Goddess.

"So you do not understand the rules that govern you."

"There are no rules," said the Goddess, "I am."

Tenesther paused for a moment, gathering her thoughts. She said, sotto voce, "Everything is property."

"Who do you belong to?" asked the Goddess, her tone light and rich like honey comb made from orange blossom.

"My people," she gestured at the Kesh frozen in time outside the circle. "We are the Families."

"When you die?"

"The rites will be observed and my spirit will be shepherded by Cyrenus."

The Goddess looked into the sky, with her chin elevated she said, "I do not know this god Cyrenus," her gaze returned to Tenesther, "What is his nature?"

"He is no god," laughed the Kesh, "he is a representation of the element of water, of command. I am of his family because that is where I excel. It is my competence. You have still not answered my question. Who ranks among your kind?"

"We are not of a kind," said the Goddess, icicles dripping from her raised arms, the smell of pepper and storms wafting from her. "There are mutual understandings. We agree with one another."

"Based on precedent," said the Kesh.

"We are mindful of what has gone before."

"Who do you belong to?"

The Goddess inclined her head. "None. I have no sides and those who walk the path are not on mine."

Oak smiled to himself, he had heard the Kesh asking these questions of believers all over the lands. The woman was playing with the Goddess, not knowing that her appearance here was unprecedented; that her taking of a human form could only have been sparked by something equally particular.

As if to underline his suspicion about the Kesh, Tenesther said, "I think you belong to the people who follow you. I think that Oak grants you substance and without him and his kind you would be little more than an idea without a home. The Fae have no need of your kind and nor do we. Neither of us have suffered as a result."

The Goddess' colour shaded darker green and butterflies flew out from her form, swirling into the air. When she spoke her voice was as thick as sap, "You say that everything is property. Perhaps you are right. Perhaps I do belong to those who follow me. It may be that we shape one another too, but if I am an idea who has found a home like a seed blown into fertile ground then ask yourself what I might become. Seeds grow into their forms and all the buffeting of the outside world will never turn a plum tree into a rose. Mortals may shape my growth but I am what I am."

"You are, however, not what you will become," said the Kesh, "What you will become utterly depends on those who remember you. Should you become forgotten will you not once again be blown on the breeze like a new born spider casting silk into the sky?"

The Goddess held a hand to stop Oak charging forward and smashing the faithless woman with his staff. "The faith that is my soil may blow away. This much is true. Yet unlike you I shall not die."

"All things die and you are not a grand cause of this world; you are a part of its fabric and one day we are promised that will fade away before returning again. It is possible you shall return then." The Kesh shrugged, "I grant you that ideas are more persistent than bone. Yet it will be a form of you. Another expression."

"So you see that I will be what I will be," said the Goddess with gentle satisfaction.

"So you see we Kesh will be what we will be. We are families and the idea of us will also persist. If the world returns then what we are, the idea we make real, will also return. We believe in ourselves. We are betrothed to our people."

Oak smiled as a realisation about Akesh sank in. *No wonder they didn't marry.* Tenesther walked over to Oak and put her arm on his shoulder. He went to shake it off but she gripped him tight; it was not a friendly gesture. "If Oak follows your path he does so only knowing some of the truth. You could give him more but I suggest it is not in your interest to let him know as he is known."

"And you know more? You see truly do you?" asked the Goddess curiously.

"Of course not, but I am judged according to my capacity, my merit and my service to my people."

"You have a faith then, faith that your people are just, that they are true in what they see. I do wonder what it is that caused your people to take such a road. I wonder if you know what that was."

"Our histories are clear," said Tenesther, "and the law is not there for 'justice' to be done."

"Ah, but so are the tales the Fae tell and who truly believes those self serving psychopaths? If the law is not there to tell you how to differentiate between right and wrong what does it exist for?"

"What do you know?" asked the woman, steel in her voice.

"More than you," said the Goddess before drawing back towards the dolmen. Shadows wrapped around her like a coat of ravens. "Ask yourself this Kesh, if you challenge the truth of my supremacy with the truth of my compatriots' existence I challenge you with the fact of your devotion to an idea that transcends yourself. If I am less than Oak would like to imagine, perhaps you should be careful that what you believe in isn't more than you have allowed for."

Tenesther stepped back, thoughtful, "I don't understand."

"At least you Kesh are honest." The Goddess looked around the circle, "So many believe they should tell me what they think I want to hear." She sighed, "As if your minds were not completely open to me."

"They like their inner secrets," said the Kesh, shrugging, "who doesn't. What more do you mean?"

The Goddess laughed, a thousand wild flowers blooming. "Are you admitting I have something you want?"

"The irony is not lost on me, but it is superficial. What I have that you want is so much more substantial than anything you might have for me."

"I will freely give you something of substance Tenesther. If you will take it," said the Goddess. "It is for your ears only and it will change everything. Are you prepared for such a burden?"

She could feel her heart beating, fear slipped through her veins. She remembered Anbaal's lessons on negotiating, that freely given was as safe as could be secured. The head of the civil service was clear on the matter, "Freely given has its own price - be prepared for that even more so than for a cost you can agree to."

"I will take your substance. Freely given."

The Goddess faded slightly and moved, without travelling, to be next to Tenesther. Oak watched as his Guide spoke secrets to the Kesh woman. He saw her eyes widen in the slit of her veil. When she was done the Goddess turned to Oak, "I have interrupted for too long my love. Let me lend my heart to your ritual, that it may be done. Circle! I hereby grant Oak my boon, do not think badly of him for taking so long to finish this rite, it was beyond him to complete it as the world demands."

"Apology accepted," said the circle and it sounded like the laments of the drowned.

"You had better finish up," said the Goddess. She indicated the Kesh, who had fallen into a crouch, "I wouldn't count on her for this. I think I have changed her." She smiled wistfully, "perhaps as much as she has changed me."

"How has she changed you?" asked Oak.

"Keep walking the path my love and perhaps, one day, you will understand what she means to me. To all of us." Then she was gone.


"Tenesther?" asked Sul as she emerged from the circle. "Tenesther - what happened in there?"

The Kesh woman looked at the man of Tyan as if seeing him for the first time, "Take me to the Firsts."

# 14 SAND AND STONE
## BY RYCH PERKINS

*The tallies must be made, the appointments must be kept.*

The ledger lay on the sandstone slab in front of the robed figure, the tables, charts and notes covering each of the precious paper pages so that not one square inch was wasted. Ink from the reservoir in the glass pen running smoothly over the rapidly filling leaves as every note was taken, every appointment made, every meeting, every delivery, each individual time and location of everything that needed to happen accounted for from memory. The Ascendant had spoken that they were leaving the harsh war torn land of Akesh and travelling to the end of the world. There was so much to do and too little sand in the hourglasses to do it.

Outside the room, the acolyte went over the lists in his own book with sweat beading on his brow. The sun had set, it being close to the end of the hours of Spirit, and the night was cool... yet still the Master's office was filled with letters and numbers, pouring from mind to page.

Drawing a deep breath and placing the small vellum notebook inside his robes, he raised his hand to knock on the block of wood hung next to the curtain that served as the door to the Master's office... such an extravagance as a wooden door would skew the tallies. As his knuckles came down, the instant before they struck the wood, the voice of the Master softly carried through the curtain, "Enter, Acolyte Rahmn."

Taking heart in the fact that he had kept exactly to the appointment time, Rahmn pushed aside the curtain and stepped inside, up to the slab of stone and simply waited. He had kept his appointment and now waited on the Master.


Merely the time it took to write the end of a word and place a full stop on the page was all the time the acolyte had to wait. Placing down the glass pen, Suli Abul, Master of Sand and Stone, Counter to the First of Command, reached  over the slab and turned over the smallest hourglass and sat upright, only his eyes visible from within his headdress.

One word was spoken, "Begin." Taking another steadying breath under the unblinking gaze of the Master, the acolyte gave his report, barely wasting any of the precious sands in the timer as he did so, the information pouring out of his memory, as he was taught since the family of NaBaal first recognised his potential as a possible Master of Sand and Stone to one of the Five.

He did not know, yet, to which family he would be

attached, there was only ever one Master for each family, the Notary of Cyrenus, who tallied every organisational appointment to the moment, fitting in everything around the short hours of the days. The Quartermaster of Tyan, the Master that moved armies, ensuring troops and equipment for war was where it was supposed to be and when it was supposed to be there. The Librarian of Kade, the Master that catalogued everything, the subject of discussions, the location of books and scrolls, the one who knew who knew what, but not necessarily the font of that information. The Broker of Cainen, that Master who knew exactly what was available and where, though he did not make the trades, he counted each ship, each cart, each sack, each ear of wheat so that it may be traded and assigned where it was needed. Or the Beholder of NaBaal, the Master who knew the power each held in the families, the magical essence that flowed through each individual, their skills and their prowess in the eldritch arts.

All of this was constantly in the back of the acolyte's mind as he made his report. He hadn't specialised yet and, as such, his mind was awhirl with the fact that his reports had to have the basics that pertained to ALL of the various things that needed accounting for and, as he spoke, he had to filter out what was useful to each Master as he reported to them. As he slipped into a troop accounting to the Notary, he stumbled... it was not necessary to give that information. Master Abul did not require it, merely the times and locations of the general staff meetings of the army commanders.

Stopping, Rahmn swallowed the lump that had

appeared in his throat.

The Master merely flicked his eyes to the timer, nearly empty, and back to the young man stood before him.

Picking up the timer, he placed it on its side, stopping the flow of time for a while. He would not scold the boy, merely instruct him. "Acolyte. Your thoughts are firm and correct. Your information and tallies accurate and concise... you merely need to catalogue them better in your mind. Take a breath and finish."

Nodding, the boy took his time to compose himself and waited until the Master restarted the flow of sand within the timer. As soon as the first grain fell through, the acolyte continued the report, giving precisely the correct information and stopping with a few grains left. Bowing his head down to show he had finished.

Returning the nod, Master of Sand and Stone, Suli Abul rose and stepped around the slab, approaching the apprentice and wrapping his arms around his shoulders, the strength in his arms surprising for one who spent so much time poring over books and timetables. Releasing Rahmn, he smiled under his headdress, "Well done. You impress me and I think I now know where you should be allocated in understudy. You shall report to the Quartermaster at the first hour of Air tomorrow. You have done well." And, with that, the apprentice's life was set on the path he had, secretly, wanted.

Stepping away, Rahmn bowed and went to speak, catching himself just in time. The one person you did NOT want to waste the time of with idle chatter was a Master of Sand and Stone. Suli recognised the start of a reply and nodded his consent, "We are in the Hollow hours, Rahmn, speak freely to me." the Master said, a rare honour given.

Taken aback for a mere moment, Rahmn quickly gathered his thoughts and spoke his piece, "Master Abul... I merely wanted to say... I thank you for seeing what I knew was my place... even though that might be presumptuous of me to say."

Chuckling, Suli Abul shook his head, "Be still, acolyte. What do we have left if we do not know where everything should be and when it should be there?

*The tallies must be made, the appointments must be kept."*

# 15 A BAD DAY FOR THE NOTARY
## BY ANDY COOK

Suli Abul, Master of sand and stone, put down his quill and stretched, it was late and Suli wanted his bed and the young local girl that was warming it for him. The room was quiet apart from Zalish talking quietly and intently to Shamshir and Tyr; the two Hands said nothing just sat and listened while the others, Suli noted, made themselves busy to avoided getting involved. Suli was not surprised as Zalish had been in such foul mood recently most sensible minded people had made themselves busy elsewhere. Suli decided to leave the Ascendant and his Hands to it and made to leave quietly when, without warning, the door to the chamber swung opened and Amar Al Fattah First of Tyan strode in.

"Victory bringer," Suli stammered, "you cannot just turn up without an appointment!" Suli froze as his brain caught up with his mouth and he involuntarily tensed as Amar turned to look at him.

"I can and I have." replied Amar quietly. Although those few words were spoken with more respect than Suli was expecting they promised the threat of extreme and swift violence if Suli wished to take the matter further. The notary wisely said nothing more.

"Amar," Zalish called, "come in and sit, the hour is late and we have much to speak of." Zalish turned and spoke quickly to both Shamshir and Tyr, too quietly for Suli to hear but they both immediately got up and, without a word or the merest glance to one their sisters, they collected their weapons and left.

Four of Amar's long strides carried the large Akeshian general over to the cushioned area where Zalish reclined; he sat, made himself comfortable and took a long pull on a shisha pipe. "Well?" asked Amar "Do we have the location?"

Zalish held up his palm, as if asking Amar to be silent, and then spoke, "Suli, fetch us some water and do not take long about it."

Suli's jaw hit the floor. He was not someone to be ordered as you would a common servant, he had earned his position, he deserved at least some respect. Why were the first of Cyrenus and the first of Tyan meeting without his knowledge (not that he cared about the content but they should have made an appointment)? Where had the Hands gone in such a hurry and why? What the fuck was going on?

"Now!" Zalish snapped and Suli, roused from his musings, hurried from the room.

Suli was cold and miserable; his torch cast little light into the darkness as it spluttered in protest against the falling rain. How he wished he had retired to his bed just a minute earlier, then none of this would have happened.

"Ho, Suli" a cheery voice called from out of the darkness. Suli looked up and saw Saiyar, scout of Kade, walking towards him.

"You're out late" Suli accused Saiyar.

"A good evening to you too, Suli. Who pissed in your water bowl?"

Suli made a sour face and waved away his own anger "It's been a long day and a bad night and I cannot see it getting any better. Anyway what brings you out at this late hour in such unpleasant weather?"

"I have returned to report back -"

"Don't tell me," Suli interrupted, "you have to report back to either Zalish or Amar."

"Yes," Saiyar replied, "how did you know?"

"Just a wild stab in the dark." Suli answered with an ironic smile, "You had better not keep them waiting, Zalish has a fierce temper again tonight and I doubt Amar is doing anything to help."


Suli collected the water and hurried back to the warmth of the room he had recently left. As he approached he saw the main doors now closed and was surprised to see the remaining three Hands now waiting in the anti-chamber; Sapah standing in front of the doors while Afsoon dozed, her head resting gently on Nizeh's lap. Suli placed the water jug on the table and sat back against the cold stone wall and closed his eyes, keeping any questions he had to himself.

"Why so miserable Notary?" asked Sapah in quiet tones.

Suli rubbed his tired and aching eyes and looked up. "Nothing really," he answered. "I am just becoming worn by the mood of the Ascendant" Sepah looked down at him, raising an eyebrow but saying nothing.

"It's not just the Ascendant" said a soft voice.

Suli looked round for the speaker and saw Azeru, the Shab who serves Amar.

"The first of Tyan has also been quite…….. difficult recently" she continued.

Suli waited for Azeru to elaborate but nothing more was forthcoming. As Suli gazed at her he realised he did not really like the Shab as a people. He was not sure why if he was honest with himself, they made him feel, well, clumsy; even the way Azeru sat on the floor was graceful. Suli sighed, closed his eyes and rested his head back against the cold stone wall.

Shortly Saiyar opened the door and stepped out into the anti-chamber.

"You can all go back in now." he said but did not stop to deliver his message, just kept moving towards the exit, Suli jumped up and moved alongside him.

"What happened in there?" Suli asked taking the scouts arm

"You know better than to ask me that." replied Saiyar looking surprised that he had even been asked the question. "I cannot stay and speak with you Suli, I have things to see done." With that the man of Kade shrugged free of Suli's grasp and left.

The Notary moved quickly back to the main room before he was shouted for. The Hands were moving to their customary position by the Ascendant; Sapah was handing him his tall red drinking glass, full of rum no doubt, while both Afsoon and Nizeh were giving Kaam none-too-pleasant looks as they pointedly moved themselves closer in to Zalish.

Bloody hell, when had she turned up? Suli felt a sudden burst of panic, what else had he missed? Why had the other two hands not returned yet? What *was* going on? Suli took a moment to calm himself and gazed around the room, he was not surprised to see AnBaal sitting quietly alongside the Victory Bringer, he'd probably been here for the whole thing anyway Suli thought. Apart from that all seemed to be as it should.

"Suli you're late with that water!" Zalish called good naturedly, "It is of no matter now anyway, the decisions have all been made, now is the time to drink late into the hollow hours"

"Tomorrow," Zalish continued as he busied himself with lighting a new pipe, "Myself and Amar will address all the Akesh, we are to leave very shortly, make sure everyone attends at the second hour of Air. These are very exciting times Suli" Zalish was speaking quickly and excitedly and Suli knew the signs of a long night ahead.

"I will return to my quarters" AnBaal said, rising. He kissed Kaam's cheek and moved towards the door. "Good luck Notary, I think you are going to need it, fire and water have a lot of catching up to get done." and with those wise, if not slightly cryptic words he handed over his glass of wine to the master of sand and stone and closed the door gently behind him.

Suli sat becoming more and more miserable as the

time passed, Zalish and Amar drank heavily and both were talking excitedly about the up and coming mission. Afsoon was fast asleep, while Sapah and Nizeh spoke quietly to each other and Kaam was long gone, declaring that if all that was going to happen was drinking then she had better things to do with her time.

All Suli could work out was that Zalish was to lead some of the Akesh on what they kept calling 'A grand adventure' while Amar would take some others somewhere else!? Each time one of them would start to talk about it, the other would drunkenly sshhh him and then they would both fall around laughing like drunken eight year olds!

Light was just starting to break the horizon when Suli walked into his chamber and slipped into bed. He gently tried to rouse the woman sleeping next to him but she would not wake, he looked at the bedside table and saw the empty wine bottle and glass on its side.

"Of course, you got pissed on cheap booze and feel asleep, bloody typical. Well at least now it cannot get any worse" Suli rolled over, blew out the candle and relaxed as sleep began to overtake him.

Haimona the huge Ghulka crashed into the court yard bellowing drunkenly, swiftly followed by three of his fellow Ghulka.

Suli's eyes snapped open.

# 16 TAX AND SPEND
## BY STEWART HOTSTON

"I'm sure your kind understand what I mean when I say the poor don't realise what a burden they can be. I'm only asking for what I've rightfully earned."

Budnazzar, third of Nabaal, watched the fat pustule of a man in front of him with growing distaste. The supplicant was dressed in stained red velvet trimmed with ermine. His outer garments had been sewn with gold thread and through the gaps he could see equally expensive under garments.

"I am a clerk. If you wish to discuss matters of trade please find a member of the Family of Cainen." he deferred.

The supplicant was silent for a moment, the tip of his tongue poking out from between waxy lips.

"You've spoken to her yes? She sent you to me?" It was all Budnazzar could do not to sigh dramatically and throw his hands into the air. Rathaz was a wily one. Perhaps, more to the point, she was as tired of all these self-entitled arseholes as he was. 'I demand. You must. This is the way it has always been done.' He was not one to question the wisdom or the competence of the Firsts but their decision to remain in this flea bitten back water of a settlement the Eored called home was one he didn't pretend to understand. The Teutonians had, by all accounts, offered the Akesh the deep port of Odessa and had been rebuffed. Odessa must have been a proper pool of worm infested camel's spit if they'd chosen this instead. He wondered if there had ever been a time when he didn't smell of horse. If there was then it was beyond his imagination to recall it clearly.

The merchant was looking at him expectantly.

"I missed that," said Budnazzar unapologetically.

"I said, I pay my taxes. I expect you people to look after us."

Budnazzar looked at the two sides of horse masquerading as men that the merchant had brought in with him - no wonder this fart at an oasis needed protecting. He wondered when the locals were going to understand that no one gave a grain of sand for this idea that everyone had to give some centralised authority a share of their wealth.

"My people," he started, and immediately regretted reflecting back to the imbecile in front of him his own prejudices, "what I mean to say, is that Akesh does not collect taxes."

"Nevertheless, I have paid them," said the merchant, quivering with indignation like a little cube of rose petal delight. "I demand you remove these squatters from my warehouse," he glowered at Budnazzar, "before I do."

"You?" spluttered the Nabaali incredulously.

"I am not without means," said the man, sitting back and folding his arms over his belly.

"I am sure you are not," said Budnazzar the same way some people used the phrase 'um' to fill space, "However, the more important question for you is who exactly did you give your taxes to? When I said we do not collect taxes that means the administrative rules now in place prohibit anyone from representing themselves as agents of Akesh property and acting on our behalf in such a manner."

The merchant was silent for a handful of breaths. Budnazzar listened placidly to the soft shifting sound of sand running through the hour glass on his desk. The fool in front of him was almost out of time. *I wonder how long before the other sandal drops?*

"I must go." the man announced suddenly. He stood, wrapped a seal skin cloak around himself and did his best to swish dramatically from the room. Budnazzar would admit that larger people could accomplish this kind of feat as well as any but the cretin leaving his office was not one of them and, in the end, only gave the impression of a drunken walrus lurching desperately for the sea.

The last grains of sand fell, one by one, through the narrow neck of the glass and suddenly his time was done. Budnazzar tidied his office, a re-floored and plastered former stables, before gathering up his paperwork and seeing himself out. *Essences save me from vested interests.*

He hurried across the main town square. Bezerek

Mizan, or Bez as they'd taken to calling their new home, was home to nearly a thousand Akesh as well as several thousand Eored, who themselves came from the other side of the continent. The natives called it something else, but he couldn't get his tongue around the apostrophes and strange soft diphthongs in their language. Bez was suitable in his view, it reminded him of the movement of a horse's tail; a sight all too common in this backwater.

He was making for his usual stop after he had satisfied his responsibilities for the day; a small inn half way between his dormitory and where the Nabaali second had set up the seat of the civil service in Bez. The truth was, they were scattered, some of the team sharing with Cyrenes and others even forced to share space with the army's quartermasters. Purple did not look good when mixed with red. *Purple and orange can be quite striking though*, he thought and made a mental note to speak to his tailor.

Budnazzar was greeted by Ashom and Liees. Ashom was dressed in tight fitting, dusty, night blue trousers and shirt in the Kesh cut, over these he had a waistcoat of lighter blue which was still clean. The man was tall as a dromedary's hump with a little tuft of blond hair to match. He wore a short beard, clipped in the latest style, even if that style came from letters which took an unknown amount of time to arrive from home.

Liees was a couple of hands shorter than Ashom and wore delicate whites whose shades varied from pale ivory through to pearl. Her base layer, the Zamass, sat loosely on the shoulders before being drawn in neatly by a wide sash around her waist. It fell from there to just below her knees. Under this she wore pyjama trews that were flared at the hips but tight around a pair of very shapely calves. A jumble of metal necklaces and bangles were worn by both, although Ashom also wore a carved wooden ring on his right index finger, an extraordinarily expensive symbol of his favour with Zaelish, the Ascendent here in the New World.

"You made it then," said Liees, a happy grin on her face.

"Sha!," said Budnazzar, "I had some buffoon demanding I clear his warehouse for him."

"Rathaz sending them to you as well?" asked Ashom as they took their ease on the blankets and cushions the landlord had laid out for them. Half the bar was set out this way while the rest remained benches and tables at waist height. Zaelish had been happy when he visited that both populations were prepared to live side by side like this. He had said 'it's in the grand tradition of the Akesh arriving that this is possible.' He'd then drunk a flask of rum, sucked on his sheesha and departed with his Hands eyeing everyone, Kesh and Eored alike, with suspicion.

None of the Eored gave them a moment's notice, although a few of the other Kesh noted their arrival with appraising looks before returning to their own conversations.

"What is the topic tonight then?" asked Liees, once the first of the flat breads and humous had been handed around.

"Governance," said Ashom. Liees rolled her eyes.

"Not again Ash." she said more kindly than her expression indicated.

"The olives the Teutonians produce are remarkably

good," said Budnazzar contentedly as the other two argued.

"Right," said Ashom, "Mr gut before good, you choose." Budnazzar held a voluptuous green, herb and oil soaked olive between his fingers and narrowed his eyes on Ashom. "Anything you want Bud. C'mon. Name your subject."

Liees opened her mouth to speak but Bud cut her off, "Tax."

"Ooooh," said Liees, "Controversial. There's not even a Cainenite here!"

"Ah. I'm not interested in debating the concept. We three are well educated enough to understand the basics. What I'm interested in is a specific case. I want to understand the power of a tax system to convey social obligations and we will consider my last supplicant of the day."

"You have us at a disadvantage," said Ashom.

Bud shook his head and explained the request of the merchant to have squatters cleared from his warehouse, "I'm not here to beat you in a debate. Rather I propose we argue the kastiq for my erstwhile self appointed pillar of the community and see if his claims hold merit under a system of taxation as he is used to and whether that should translate somehow into our preferred, and undoubtedly superior, style of self governance."

"Ok, who takes which roles?" asked Liees, dabbing at the corner of her mouth with a cloth before washing her hands in the bowl of warm water in the middle of their rug.

"Much as it pains me, I shall have to represent the merchant," said Budnazzar.

"I'll adjudicate," said Ashom.

"Fine by me," said Liees, "I like showing up these fools."

"So begin," said Ashom.

Budnazzar sat back against the low roll of cushion and popped a small square of almond and honey cake into his mouth. Tucking it into his cheek he said, "We all understand that if each gives a little of what he accrues to a central pot then all can benefit from luxuries that otherwise no single individual would be able to create. I'm not interested in discussing how this is obviously superior to every person claiming they're the fount of their own success. What I am here to say is that this relationship forms a kind of contract between all people, richest or poorest, and that those who give more, in an absolute sense, help create an environment that all, including themselves, enjoy.

"Given this I would say that I shall argue that if a tax system is to work then none can be allowed to opt out and all should expect, as a result of their participation, to receive certain goods in exchange for their investment."

The other two sat quietly, Liees' expression one of impending triumph. Bud hoped he could make it difficult for her. "Now, some say that tax is a burden - they are clearly idiots. Tax is an investment in all our goods - even if we don't all use those goods equally. It is the very fact of their ubiquity that makes them a good and we should focus now on my justifications.

"First. I submit that I, yon merchant with a large belly from too many slices of boar, have paid my dues. On an absolute basis I have paid more than nine out of ten people in this horse infested berg added together. As such I would hold the right that the rule of law be upheld on my behalf. If you deny me my incentive for contributing to a system into which I give more than I take I can easily withdraw myself to the detriment of all.

"Second. Through my greater giving I am worth more than those who contribute nothing or are not as skilled or effective as me. I submit that the law should be upheld in my case especially because it would take ten ordinary workers to give the same good as I do by myself.

"Third. I can, if help is not forthcoming, take the matter into my own hands. I am a man of means and could shape the law according to my own ends. We all agree that this would be a bad thing but even if we admit that I should not have the law at my fingertips we also forget that doing so is not simply a matter of the risks that might arise from the abuse of the law, but because it's a lever that prises apart the edifice of the social good completely. It is a bad thing and to avoid that I submit that you must see to my needs."

Ashom drummed his fingers on the table in appreciation of Bud's justifications.

"Liees. It is your turn."

The woman tucked a strand of hair behind a tiny ear and sucked in the corner of her bottom lip. "I object to all your justifications. I shall start with the last first.

"First challenge. The people will not stand for you taking the matter into your own hands. Akesh holds the right to violence within its own purview and will treat any who seek to exercise harm on others without justification to such a lesson that the people will be both instructed and satisfied over the consequences of your transgression. Your third justification is a threat and we, the people, will treat you as we would treat any who threaten us. On that basis I cannot be persuaded by your argument.

"Second challenge. Akesh distinguish only by competence, not by possessions material or political. None is worthy of special treatment. Your own concept allows that all could, and by your own words, should be treated equally to these goods held in common by the people. It is not an imperative, I can easily imagine a system of tax where just a minority enjoyed the fruits of other people's tax, but that is not what you've presented to us. Your second justification is that you are, because of your physical wealth, better than others. Akesh does not recognise this. Even the most competent are only rewarded with extra responsibility. You have not asked for responsibility but for a lower burden of proof before the people jump to your every whim. I find that your second justification cannot be upheld for you, or for anyone else. The foundation of the claim is flawed and hence rejected.

"Third. This is the same justification as the third and as such I reject it on the same basis." Liees folded her arms, a large toothy smile covering her face challenging him to come back at her.

"Bud, do you accept these challenges?" asked Ashom.

"No. I would challenge the last first."

Ashom nodded his consent. Around the room Eored and Akesh alike had quieted down and were listening to the argument. Budnazzar loved an audience, he was always cheered when he thought he had a chance to remind people why the way of Akesh was the best any nation had yet devised.

"If you do not see to my needs and force me to take matters into my own hands then not only is society diminished in that moment - in its failure to live up to its side of the bargain, but if I do not act to protect my own goods then we are all diminished. In forcing me to act, you force me to act outside of the society. You force me into the status of an outsider; someone to be afraid of, to be controlled and to be managed. Why? Because you failed to rectify the first wrong I am now the 'bad guy'. It is no plea but a cry for help and a desperate act forced upon me by the failure of the authority who collected my money and did not help me when I needed it. Saying you'll make an example of me will only encourage those who put me into this position in the first place; it is rewarding incompetence."

Liees nodded approvingly and even Ashom smiled. "Excellent rebuttal Budnazzar."

They went backwards and forwards for another hour, the pastries and rum gradually dwindling as they batted the arguments around. The inn had filled up during the course of their discussion, but newcomers found all attention was directed at these three Kesh. Occasionally someone would move to interrupt but was forcefully silenced by those in the circle of observers closest to the Kastiq.

Budnazzar was pleased; it was an excellent exercise to defend a point he did not remotely believe in. As far as he was concerned the Kesh were organised along superior lines. They did not need money and they did not tax. Their structure along lines of competence meant that all members of the nations of Akesh owed each other their service as they were able to deliver. The physical wealth of the Cainanites was balanced by the knowledge of Kade and the power of Nabaal. They in turn were checked by Cyrenus' exercise of control and Tyan's grasp of the nature of conflict, the harnessing of raw energy for the creation of order. If one had needs they were met first by family and then by Akesh. If roads needed building the families would work together to build them - from the recognition of need to the laying of the last stone and the celebration afterwards.

*These problems wouldn't arise in Akesh*, he thought contentedly to himself.

He actually thought they might have to retire without deciding on the outcome. Liees wasn't pushing quite as hard as he thought she could, and he suspected she was passing over a couple of the more obvious lines of attack deliberately. It didn't occur to him that it was because of how she felt about him, the woman was seeing some giant of a Tyanite with whose physicality he was sure he couldn't compare. *I suppose it could be because the most obvious lines of attack would be those most upsetting to our hosts here in Bez.* He shrugged inwardly; he didn't care but could understand why she would want to put on a good show for them, to help them feel the Kesh truly considered their ways carefully. Sometimes destroying another's arguments too easily left them suspecting there was more to be said, as if the brevity itself conveyed a lack of closure on the matter.

They decided to see to their needs and broke up for a few minutes. Upon their return, Bud found Ashom stood in the centre of their rug talking to a local man, dressed in stiffened leather armour over green and brown cloth. One of the Eored's men at arms. Akesh had not required or thought to presume the disarmament of the local population when they had accepted the role of administrators of the town. In turn, the Eored had not mentioned the lack of conversation about the means to conduct war but had quickly sought out the Tyanites and, together, they had arranged a new state of policing and managing the issues that arose which could conceivably require an armed response. So far nothing had happened to test this new relationship. Rumour was they had grown comfortable with the different ways each side went to battle; strategies had been developed to harness the effectiveness of both sides as an integrated unit. Ashom was laconic about it but claimed the Tyanites were only following standing orders laid out in the manuals on assimilating host populations.

Ashom waved Bud over before he could relax.

"This man, Alfeod, has something you should listen to," said Ashom, his expression grave.

Budnazzar sighed, he had heard about the Firsts opening the Kastiq to non-Kesh, but was not an admirer of the practice. "Yes. Carry on." He waved his hand in a desultory fashion.

"You've been discussing the warehouse by the harbour?" asked the man who seemed to Bud like a half shaved bear in a suit of armour.

He nodded, "well not as such, we were discussing what should be done about it. Whether it was appropriate to respond to the owner's demands for us to interfere and whether the fact that he'd foolishly paid a blaggard his 'taxes'." Here he put his fingers in the air to indicate he regarded taxes as ridiculous, "meant he could demand we act."

"That's nice," said Alfeod, "That means you'll want to know that his warehouse is on fire and he has ten men stood outside the entrances armed to the teeth ready to cut up any who escape."

The room was silent.

Budnazzar started to sweat, "I'm not sure how this concerns us." he said, hoping he sounded convincing.

"Not for me to say," said the soldier, "just that the Tyanites said you'd want to come down as it's the only place in town where your papers and records are being stored." The man looked as if the warehouse could happily char to the ground before he would even go take a look, but at the news of Nabaali records burning Budnazzar felt his stomach turn over.

Liees and Ashom were watching him and in their eyes he saw his own fear. "I should go." he said meekly.

"We should come," said Liees. Others around the room were already gathering their shawls and outer robes. Bud swallowed hard and led the way.

It took a turn of the Tre glass, the third size of sand timer, to reach the warehouse. It took only half that time for the blaze to light up the sky with an orange grasping for the heavens. A detachment of Tyanites and Eored met him halfway. He recognised the leader of his own people, a wiry man of steel called Emmek Nadur.

"What has happened?" he asked.

Emmek shook his head as if the world had forgone common sense, "Some lunatic set fire to his own warehouse. Now he refuses to let anyone out." He looked at Budnazzar as if it were all his fault. His Eored counterpart stood off to the side, listening but polite enough not to look like he was taking it all in.

"Is this how we usually handle public disturbances?" asked Bud, his voice breaking with the stress.

"Of course not clerk," said Emmek, "but this chap said he had permission to do with his property whatever he wanted to. I'm no scholar of the law but I have to say that seems within the realms of the justified."

"That warehouse is the hall of Nabaal's records," said Bud furiously, "It is not just his property that's at stake." Even in the inconstant flickering of the blaze he saw the man blanche. "Who gave this permission?"

Suddenly Nadur seemed more certain, "You did."

"I most certainly did not," he said, racking his brain just in case. It was claims like this that could make a man doubt his own sanity.

"He said that you agreed that he had the means to do as he wished. He is doing as he wishes with his means. Are you saying I should have stopped him?"

*It's not my fault you sodden rat of a man,* thought Bud. "Did he have a signed checklist?"

It was Emmek's turn to swallow hard. "Well. No. But you said."

"I said something that bastard son of a walrus did not understand. Perhaps wilfully. You have failed to ask him for the checklist. You need to stop him. Stop him now. Then you need to wake Cyrenus' mages up so they can stop this fire."

Emmek turned on his heel and ran for his men. Within moments they were running in all directions.

Budnazzar turned to Liees, relief lifting his heart somewhat. Even if they lost the records he wouldn't be blamed.

Liees was looking at him with a curious expression her face. "What?" he asked.

"This is your fault." she said calmly. "You were so set on treating this man's demands according to his own standards that you forgot what you should have done, what any Kesh should have done."

He ground his teeth, "And what was that?"

"You should have made sure of the common good."

"You cannot be serious." he said, but he knew she was. Each and every one of the Kesh around him had the same look on their faces. His incompetence was to blame.

"I call you to Kastiq," said Liees and he knew that this time she would not pass over his flaws.

# ABOUT THE AUTHORS

Bex Cardnell - Bex has a life goal of replacing the need for cavity wall insulation in her home with yarn. When not doing science she can be found in the kitchen, or the lounge, or bedroom, or pub, or a field, or somewhere else in fact. But never found in a game of hide and seek.

Richard George - The author of this story is an enigma, wrapped up in a mystery cloaked in myth... Or some other lie, you choose. Either way enjoy the story.

Andy Smith - Andy grew up on a steady diet of Star Trek, Anne McCaffrey and Tolkein, so it was only a matter of time before he escaped his school, university and work into story writing, roleplaying and, eventually the Akesh. Turning up with barrel after barrel of "Tyanabad Red" wine probably didn't hurt things either. When not being Suhrab, the wise and no nonsense vintner (or his new project, the Human Immovable Object), Andy can be found drinking real ale, being sat on by his parent's dogs or his nephew, or asleep.

Ben Hesketh - Ben is a repressed renaissance man. With dreams that outstrip even his amazing abilities, its a surprise that he isn't famously doing something more with his life. The angry beard of the Akesh who just needs a hug. In reality Ben works, does stuff and lives in the cold north. Rumours he is Batman are only founded in his own brain.

Stewart Hotston - Stewart has been practising his Grand Vizier sneer for the last decade or so. It was only when the Akesh came along that his life-long dream of wearing purple robes and looking like Ming the Merciless became a reality. In a life studded with the bizarre, the tragic and the comedic he regards the chance to write and edit as both therapy and safety valve.

Rych Perkins – 33 year old male that thinks he's 23, living in Northampton with his three cats Frog, Voodoo and Sausage. Started LARPing for something to break the boredom of working for Games Workshop when he was 18 and hasn't looked back since. He takes a small teddy bear to every event he goes to. The bear is called Cuddles and has his own Twitter page followed by Barack Obama, the Hoff and Alyssa Milano.

Si Campbell-Wilson - Simon found he had a passion for the fantasy worlds at a young age, having read Tolkien's Lord of the Rings and discovering a certain table top battle game that shall remain nameless for legal reasons. Later in life Simon went into media production and is now a graphic designer, but he never left his love of reading fantasy novels and finally put pen to paper for the first time with this short story. So either a very brave or very kind editor has decided the masses should have a read!

Andy Cook – Bambi-ankled, rum-drinking spacktard. No more needs to be said.

Jen Smith – Jen Smith is 26 and works in financial

services. She is the winner of such awards as 'Kirklees Young Writer 2005', 'Best Gunman' and 'Most Surprising Display of Competence in the face of Own Ineptitude'. In the Kesh she plays gentle-spirited handmaiden Afsoon.

Printed in Great Britain
by Amazon.co.uk, Ltd.,
Marston Gate.